JONDELLE

'Earth,' she mused. 'A place?'
'A world. My world.'

'Could a planet have such a name?'
Her voice was light. 'It's like calling a world
sand or dirt or ground. This is earth.' Her
hand touched the soil. 'But we call this place
Ourelle.'

'Earth is real', Dumarest insisted. 'A world,
old and scarred by ancient wars. The stars are
few and there is a great, single moon which
hangs like a pale sun in the night sky.'

'A legend,' she said. 'I have heard of them.
Worlds which have never existed. Jackpot
and Bonanza, El Dorado, and Camelot. Eden
too, though I think there is an actual planet
called that.'

'There are three,' he said bleakly. 'And there
could be more. But there is only one Earth
and I was born on its surface. One day I shall
find it.'

Also in Arrow by E. C. Tubb

E. C. Tubb

Jondelle

ARROW BOOKS

Arrow Books Limited
3 Fitzroy Square, London W1

An imprint of the Hutchinson Publishing Group

London Melbourne Sydney Auckland
Wellington Johannesburg and agencies
throughout the world

First published in Great Britain by Arrow Books Ltd 1977
© E. C. Tubb 1973

Made and printed in Great Britain
by The Anchor Press Ltd
Tiptree, Essex

ISBN 0 09 914490 5

CHAPTER

ONE

Akon Batik was an old man with a seamed face and slanting eyes flecked with motes of amber. His lobeless ears were set close to his rounded skull and his thin mouth curved downward as if he had tasted the universe and found it not to his liking. He wore an embroidered robe of black and yellow, the wide sleeves falling low over his hands. A round cap of matching color was adorned by a single jewel which caught the light and reflected it in splinters of lambent ruby. Casually he stirred the heap of crystals lying before him on the solid desk of inlaid woods. His finger was thin, hooked, the nail long and sharply pointed. At its touch the crystals made a dry rustling as they shifted over the sheet of paper on which they lay.

"From Estale?"

"Yes," said Dumarest. "From Estale."

"A hard world," mused the jeweler. "A bleak place with little to commend it aside from the workings which produce its wealth. A single vein of lerad in which are to be found the chorismite crystals." He touched them again, watching as they turned, his eyes remote. "I understood the company mining them was jealous of its monopoly."

"It is."

"And yet you have a score of them."

It was more of a question than a statement but one which Dumarest had no intention of answering. He leaned back in his chair looking again at the paneled walls, the painted ceiling, the rugs of price which lay scattered on the floor. Light shone in a yellow flood from recessed lanterns, soft, gentle, lulling with implied warmth and comfort. It was hard to remember that this room lay within a fortress of stone, harder still to bear in mind that not all the defenses were outside. There would be men, perhaps, watching, electronic devices certainly, means to protect and to kill if the need arose. Akon Batik had not grown old in his trade by neglecting elementary precautions.

He said, "Why did you bring them to me?"

"You have a reputation," said Dumarest. "You will buy what is offered. Of course, if you are not interested in the crystals I will waste no more of your time."

"Did I say that?" Again the long nail touched the little heap. "But it is in my nature to be curious. I wonder how a man could manage to elude the guards and the inspection at the field on Estale. A man working the vein could no doubt manage to retain a few crystals—but to leave with them?"

"They are genuine."

"I believe you, but my eyes are not as young as they were and it would be well to make certain." The jeweler switched on a lamp and bathed the surface of his desk with invisible ultraviolet. The crystals blazed with a shimmering kaleidoscope of color, rainbows painting the seamed cheeks, the slanted eyes, glowing from the dark wood of the paneled walls. For a long moment he stared at them, then switched off the lamp. "Chorismite," he said. "There can be no doubt."

Dumarest said, "You will buy them?"

The crux of the matter, but Akon Batik was not to be hurried. He leaned back, eyes thoughtful as he studied his visitor. A hard man, he decided, tall, lean, somber in his clothing. Pants tucked into high boots, the hilt of a knife riding above the right. A tunic with long sleeves caught at the wrists and high about the throat. Clothing of a neutral gray and all of it showing the marks of hard usage, the plastic scratched and scuffed with minor attritions. His eyes lifted to the face, studying the deep-set eyes, the determined set of the jaw, the firm mouth which could easily become cruel. The face of a man who had early learned to survive without the protection of House or Guild or Organization.

A traveler. A man who moved from world to world in search of something, or perhaps because he was unable to rest. A wanderer who had seen a hundred worlds and found none he could call his own.

Quietly he said, "Estale is a bad world and not one a traveler should visit. There would be little opportunity for such a man to work and collect the price of a passage. You agree?"

There were many such, dead-end planets, end-of-the-line worlds devoid of industry, poverty-stricken cultures in which a stranded traveler stood no chance of making an escape. Dumarest had seen too many of them. Bleakly he nodded.

"On Estale you work in the mine or you do not work," continued the jeweler. "And, once you sign the contract, escape is rare. The pay is low, prices high, a worker remains constantly in debt. Yet a shrewd man could beat the system. A man who saved every coin, who indulged in no pleasures, and who wasted no opportunity in order to build his stake. A man who would bide his time, work out his contract, and leavé without suspicion." He paused and added, softly, "And who would suspect that a man riding Low would have a fortune hidden within his person."

And his visitor had ridden Low; the signs were plain. No body fat, a drawn appearance about the eyes, the hands thinner than nature intended. The result of riding doped, frozen, and ninety percent dead in caskets designed for the transportation of beasts. Risking the fifteen percent death rate for the sake of cheap travel.

"Will you buy the crystals?"

"I will give you one thousand stergals for them," said Akon Batik flatly, and translated the sum into more recognizable terms. "That is the cost of two High passages."

Dumarest frowned. "They are worth more."

"Far more," agreed the jeweler. "But commissions will have to be paid and you are selling, not buying. My profit will be little more than what I pay you—but you need have no fears once you leave my house. A thousand stergals. You agree?"

He smiled as Dumarest nodded, a quirk of the lips, more a grimace than an expression of amusement. Yet his voice held satisfaction as he said, "The money will be given to you as you leave. And now, a glass of wine to seal the bargain. You have no objection?"

It was tradition, Dumarest guessed, a ritual which politeness dictated he should share. And, perhaps, things could be learned over the wine.

It was dark, thick, and heavy with a cloying sweetness, pungent with the scent of spice which warmed throat and stomach. Cautiously he sipped and then said, casually, "You have lived long and are wise. Tell me: have you ever heard of a planet called Earth?"

"Earth?" Akon Batik stared thoughtfully at his wine.

"An odd name for a world, but no, I have not. A place you seek?"

"A world I intend to find."

"May good fortune attend you. Do you intend to remain long on Ourelle?"

"I don't know," said Dumarest cautiously. "It depends."

"On whether or not you find things to attract you?" The jeweler sipped at his wine. "I asked because it is barely possible that I may be able to find you suitable employment. Men who can acquire chorismite are rare. It could be that I will have a proposition to make you at some later time. Naturally, it will be of a profitable kind. You would not be averse?"

"I would be interested," said Dumarest flatly. He sipped again at his wine, wondering at the other's interest. A man like Akon Batik would not have a need for men to do his bidding; certainly he would not have to rely on strangers no matter how skillful they appeared to be. Setting down the goblet, he said, "I thank you for the wine and your courtesy. And now, the money?"

"It's waiting for you at the door." The jeweler pursed his thin mouth. "You are a stranger on Ourelle, am I correct?"

"Yes."

"It is a strange world and perhaps I could save you misfortune. If you are tempted to seek games of chance, do not play in the Stewpot, the Pavilion of Many Delights, or the Purple Flower. You may win, but you will not live to count your gains. The House of the Gong is as fair as any and you will be safe from violence."

Dumarest said, "You own it?"

"Naturally, and if you are eager to lose your money, I may as well regain what I have paid. Another thing: Ourelle is not as other worlds. If you remain in the city, that need not concern you; but if you wish to explore, take nothing for granted. You have plans?"

"To look around. To see that is to be seen. You have a museum? A scientific institute?"

The jeweler blinked his surprise. "We have a House of Knowledge. The Kladour. You will recognize it by the fluted spire. It is the pride of Sargone. And now, if you would care for more wine? No? Then our business is completed. If the need arises, I shall contact you. In the meantime, good fortune attend each step you take."

"And may your life be full of gladness," responded Dumarest, and knew by the sudden shift of light in the slanted eyes that he had enhanced his standing in the jeweler's estimation. A man who insisted on wine to complete a transaction would be sensitive to such courtesies.

A moving arrow of dull green guided him through a labyrinth of passages to the outer door where a squat man handed him a bag of coins, waiting phlegmatically as Dumarest counted them. The money safe in his pocket, he stepped into the street, blinking at the comparative brilliance of the late afternoon. An emerald sun hung low in the sky, painting the blank facades of the buildings with a dozen shades of green; dark in shuttered windows and enigmatic doors, bright and pale on parapets and trailing vines heavy with blossoms of blue, gold, and scarlet. Above the roofs, seemingly close, he could see a peculiar spire twisting as it rose to terminate in a delicate shaft topped by a gilded ball. The Kladour, he guessed, and made his way toward it.

In Sargone no street could be called straight. Every alley, avenue, road, and byway was curved, a crescent, the part of circle, the twist of a spiral, all wending in baffling contradiction as if designed by the undulations of a gigantic serpent. A guide had taken him to the jeweler's house, another would have taken him to the Kladour, but the street had been empty and the spire deceptively close. Dumarest had trusted to his own ability and soon found that he was completely lost.

He halted, trying to orient himself. The sun was where it should be, the spire too, but it was more distant now and the street in which he stood wended in the wrong direction. Traffic was light and pedestrians few. An alley gave onto a more populous street which irritatingly sent him away from his objective.

A man rubbed his chin, his eyes sharp as Dumarest asked directions.

"The Kladour? Hell, man, you won't find nothing there. You want the Narn. Everything to satisfy a man in the Narn. Girls, wine, gambling, sensitapes, analogues—you name it and it's to be had. Fights too. You like to watch a good fight? Ten-inch blades and to the death. Tell you what—you hire me and I'll take you to where you want to go."

A tout eager to make a commission. Dumarest said, "Forget it. I want the Kladour."

"First right, second right, first left, third left, straight ahead. If you change your mind and hit the Narn, ask for Jarge Venrush. If you want action, I can show you all you can use. Remember the name. You'll find me in the Disaphar."

Dumarest nodded and moved on. The second on the right was a narrow alley thick with emerald shadows, a gash cut between high buildings and prematurely dark. He trod softly, keeping to the center, ears strained with instinctive caution. Something rattled ahead and he tensed as a shape darted from behind a can. A small animal seeking its prey; lambent eyes glowed as he passed where it crouched, feeding. Beyond it, the the left-hand turn showed an opening little wider than the alley.

He slowed as he neared it, his skin prickling with primitive warning. It was too dark, too convenient for any who might choose to lie in wait, and the tout could have sent him into a trap. Sargone was a city no better than any other. It had its dark corners and own species of savage life. Men who lived on helpless prey. Robbers and those who would find it more convenient to kill from a distance.

Dumarest halted, then turned to retrace his steps, halting again as he heard the cry.

It was high, shrill, more of a scream than a shout, and it came from the opening behind. He spun, one hand dropping to the knife in his boot, the nine-inch blade glowing emerald as he lifted it from its sheath, faded sunlight bright on needle point and razor edge. Two steps and he had reached the opening, was racing down the alley as the cry came again. A woman, he thought, a girl, then corrected the impression as he saw the tableau ahead. Not a girl, a child, a small boy pressed tight against a wall.

He wasn't alone. Beside him stood a man, thickset, his hair a tangled darkness, his face drawn and reflecting his fear. His hands were clenched in baffled helplessness as he faced the three standing close. They were decked and masked, glittering tunics bright with a variety of symbols, the masks grotesque with beak and horn. Camouflage or protection—it was impossible to see what lay beneath the masks, but Dumarest had no doubt as to what they intended. Robbers, armed with knives, willing and perhaps eager to use them against defenseless victims. To cut and stab and slash in a fury of blood-lust. To kill the man and perhaps the boy. Degenerates out for a little fun. The scum inevitable in any civilization.

One turned as he approached. Dumarest saw the mask, the glitter of eyes, the sweep of the blade held like a sword in a gloved hand. It lanced forward in an upswinging thrust which would have disemboweled an uprotected belly. Dumarest jumped to one side, his own blade whining as it cut through the air, the edge hitting, biting, breaking free as it slashed through the hand just behind the fingers. Fingers and knife fell in a fountain of blood, the blade swinging up again in a return slash at the lower edge of the mask, the tip finding and severing the soft tissues of the throat.

Without pause, he sprang at the nearest of the other two, left arm blocking the defending blade, his own point lifting to aim at an eye, to thrust, twist, and emerge dripping with fresh blood.

"Hold it!" The third man had retreated, dropping his knife, his hand now heavy with the weight of a gun. "You fool," he said. "You interfered. No one asked you to do that. All we wanted was the kid. You could have walked past and forgotten what you'd seen. Instead you had to act the hero. Well, now you're going to pay for it." He poised the weapon. "In the belly," he said. "A hole burned right through your guts. You'll take a long time to die and scream every minute of it. Damn you! Here it comes!"

Dumarest moved, leaping to one side, his arm reaching back, than forward, the knife spinning from his hand. He saw the mask, the gun, the ruby guide-beam of the laser, and caught the stench of seared plastic and metal. Pain tore at his side and then the beam had gone, the gun swinging upward, the mask, the hilt of the knife protruding like an ugly growth from the flesh beneath.

Then pain became a consuming nightmare.

CHAPTER

TWO

He looked to be six pushing seven, a stocky lad with a mane of yellow hair and eyes deep-set and vividly blue. His back and shoulders were straight, his stomach still rotund from early fat, his hands dimpled, his mouth a soft rose. He stood beside the bed, very solemn, his words very precise.

"My name is Jondelle. I must thank you for having saved me when we were attacked in the city."

Big words for a small boy, thought Dumarest, but, equally solemn, he said, "It was my pleasure to be of service. Can you tell me what happened?"

"After you were shot?"

"Yes."

"Elray saved you. He helped you to our raft and brought you back home. I didn't forget to bring your knife. Do you want it now?"

"Please," said Dumarest.

"I've cleaned it," said the boy. "It was all sticky with blood but I washed it and polished it. Have you used it to kill many men?"

"No more than I had to."

"I saw how you threw it. Will you teach me how to throw a knife?"

"Perhaps." Dumarest sat upright on the cot. He was naked beneath the sheets, a transparent bandage tight against the left side of his body. Beneath the covering he could see the flesh almost totally healed. Hormones, he thought, or perhaps even slow-time, the magic chemical which speeded the metabolism so that a man lived a day in a few minutes. But he doubted it. The use of slow-time brought ravenous hunger and he did not feel that. And there were no marks on his arms to show the use of intravenous feeding.

"Makgar nursed you," said the boy. "She is very good at that, but I think Weemek helped."

"Weemek?"

"A friend who visits us sometimes. If you stay here, you will meet him. I call it a 'him,' but I can't be sure. He isn't human, you see."

Dumarest didn't, but he didn't correct the boy. He leaned back, faintly amused and more than a little puzzled. The lad spoke too precisely for his apparent age as if he'd had intensive schooling during his formative years. Or perhaps it was normal for childern of this culture to be so forward.

He said, "May I have my knife now?"

It was clean as the boy had said, the edge freshly honed, the steel polished.

"And my clothes?"

"Makgar has those. She has refurbished them. Is there anything else you want?"

Information, but that could wait. Dumarest shook his head, and as the boy left looked around. He was in a room made of slabbed stone, the ceiling low and heavily beamed, the floor of wood smoothed to a natural polish. Rugs softened the spartan simplicity, a few prints made bright patches of color against the walls, and a broad window was bright with a pale green light. The sun was high over rolling plains and fields thick with crops. Trees stood at the crest of a distant ridge and a narrow river wended down a slope to vanish in a curve which led beyond the house.

A farmhouse, he guessed. The center of an agricultural complex. Somewhere would be barns for livestock, silos for storage, sheds for machinery. Other houses also for the workers. He opened the window and breathed deeply of the air. It was warm, scented with unfamiliar odors, rich and invigorating. Suddenly he was hungry.

"You shouldn't be up," said a voice behind him. "Get back into bed now."

He turned and looked at the woman. She was tall, with a closely cut mane of dark hair, her dark eyes holding a hint of amusement and something of anticipation. Her figure was full and lush beneath a dress of some brown fabric belted at the waist. He feet were bare in leather sandals, her hands broad, the fingers long and tapered. The hands of a sculpter, he thought, or those of a surgeon. Unabashed by his nakedness, he stood and met her eyes.

"Bed," she repeated. "Immediately."

"You are Makgar?"

"Yes, but I am also your doctor, your nurse, and your hostess. Also I am very grateful and would hate to see you suffer a relapse. If it hadn't been for the protective mesh buried in your clothing, the beam of that laser would have killed you. As it was the heat was dissipated just enough to slow penetration. Now please get into bed."

He obeyed, conscious of a sudden weakness.

"How long have I been here?"

"Ten days. You lost a great deal of blood, but that I was able to replace. However, you were greatly debilitated, no fat and showing signs of long-standing malnutrition. I've had you under hypnotic sedation and used fast-acting hormones to promote rapid healing. I would have used slow-time, but, frankly, you were in no condition to take it." She paused, hesitating, and he guessed at her question.

"Six months working in a mine and skimping on food," he said dryly. "Then riding Low. It isn't the best way to stay in condition."

"I wondered," she said. "Thank you for confiding in me."

"You are the doctor—you need to know." He added, quietly, "You mentioned hypnotic sedation."

"A technique of my own. You felt no pain and were able to eat at regular intervals, but your privacy remained inviolate, Earl." She smiled at his expression. "Some things I had to know—your name for one. For therapeutic reasons, not official. We don't bother with such things here at Relad."

"The farm?"

"The area. At times you became a little delirious and the use of your name enabled me to strengthen your libido. Anyway, that is all over now. Good food and rest will make you as good as new."

"As my clothes?"

"You know?"

"The boy told me that you were refurbishing them. A big word for a small boy to use."

"He is a very unusual boy." She swallowed and added, "I am not good at displaying emotion, my training perhaps, but there it is. And some things are impossible to put into words. But know this. Anything I have, anything you want, is yours for what you did. Had Jondelle been taken—"

"He wasn't," said Dumarest.

"Elray was helpless. You mustn't blame him. He would die for the boy but—"

"He isn't a killer," said Dumarest flatly. "And against three men with knives what could he have done? Died, perhaps, and would that have saved the boy?"

"You saved him. Are you a killer?" She didn't wait for an answer. "No, you may have killed in your time but only in order to survive. And you are no stranger to violence; the scars on your body told me that. Knife scars, Earl—there can be no mistake. I've seen them before on men who fought in the ring."

Fought and killed to the roaring of a blood-hungry crowd. He smelled again the scent of blood, the taint of the air heavy with anticipation, saw the animal stare from civilized masks as cultured men and women screamed for violent death. The catharsis demanded by societies grown decadent, the chance for a traveler to make a stake, a young man a reputation.

"A man accustomed to violence," she said softly. "But more than that. Elgar told me of your speed, the incredible way in which you moved. To throw a knife as fast as a man can pull a trigger! To send it across twenty feet before the beam could reach you. Had it been less, you would not have been burned. You are no ordinary man, Earl Dumarest, but I thank all the gods that ever were that you were at that place at that time."

Her voice betrayed her. Impassive though her face remained, the tones carried a vibrant note of raw emotion. Another woman would have burst into tears, caught his hand, perhaps, even showed signs of hysteria. And it was more than simple gratitude. It was as if a terrible fear had been realized and the reaction remained, all the more strong because of thoughts of what might have been.

He knew that he could reach for her, touch her, and whatever he desired would be freely given. Instead he said, "Those men wanted to take the boy. Do you know why?"

She drew a deep, shuddering breath. "Ransom, perhaps?"

"Not unless you are rich," he said dryly. "Are you?"

"We have the farm and little else. You carry more money than we own."

"Assets, then? Is the farm of value?"

"Land is cheap on Ourelle. We have food and live well, but that is about all."

"Enemies?"

"No. None that I know of."

He said, flatly, "Someone for some reason wanted to kidnap your boy. He is your son, I take it?"

"The child of my body," she said. "Yes."

"Those men weren't there by accident," he said. "They knew what they wanted and where to find it. Does Elray often take the lad into the city?"

"No. Not often. He went to collect a part for one of the machines and thought Jondelle would be interested. They had walked for a while, at random, sight-seeing and visiting the Kladour. A normal day for any man to spend with a young boy. And then, as they were making toward the place where they had left the raft, those men attacked them. They must have intended robbery. When you appeared the one with the gun must have hoped you would believe him. A warning perhaps."

"Perhaps," he said.

"It had to be that. Why should anyone want to steal a boy? How would they know where to find him if they did? It was a coincidence—it had to be."

Dumarest doubted it, but one thing was obvious. It was a subject she had no wish to discuss with a stranger and it was none of his business. And he had no desire to become involved. The boy was not alone. He had his mother and a man who appeared to be his father, though the fact hadn't been clearly stated. He had a farm on which to live and there would be retainers of a kind, workers, those dependent on the owners, obligated to defend both life and property. The protection of a House, small though that House might be. And here, at least, he was isolated from the dangers of the city.

More protection than Dumarest had ever known. More comfort and security and certainly more love. He leaned back on the pillows, dreaming, remembering a time best forgotten when hunger had been a constant companion and rocks and stones his only playthings.

Makgar said, "You are tired. The boy woke you too soon and your wound is far from healed. I shall send you food and you will rest and soon will be well again. Need I say that you are welcome to stay as long as you wish?"

"You are kind."

"Not kind, selfish. You give this place strength and I—" She broke off, then resumed in a more casual tone. "I am a doctor and do not want to see my work wasted. You are ready to eat?"

There were steaks, thick and almost raw, seared on beds of charcoal, served with eggs and mounds of butter. He ate and slept and woke to eat again, a high-protein diet designed to restore lost energy and to replace the fat consumed during the past few months. In two days he was on his feet, taking long walks over the fields and working at laborious tasks in order to tone muscle and sinew. And with him, almost constantly, was the boy.

He was very solemn, dressed in dark brown pants and shirt, thick boots on his small feet, and a loop of beads hung around his neck. They were large, each the size of a small egg, brightly colored, and strung on a length of wire with the strong metal knotted between each bead. Seeds, thought Dumarest, the product of some exotic plant, attractive to the eye and amusing to a child. Yet at times it was hard to think of Jondelle as a child. His words were too precise, his manner too adult.

"How do you make sure the blade hits in the same place every time?" he asked as he watched Dumarest chop a log. "When I tried to do it, I hit all over the place."

"You aim with the haft of the ax," said Dumarest. "The point near your hands. The blade follows."

"Can you throw an ax as you can a knife?"

Dumarest glanced at a trunk lying several yards to one side. He hefted the ax, feeling its balance, then threw it with a sudden release of energy. The blade bit deeply into the wood.

"I wish I could do that," said the boy. "Will you teach me?"

"You can't be taught. You can be shown, then the rest is up to you. It's a matter of balance and judging distance. That and plenty of practice."

"The knife, then. Will you help me to learn how to throw a knife? To use one?"

"Your father should do that."

"Elray isn't my father. He married Makgar, but that is all."

It was confirmation of what Dumarest had suspected. Two dark-haired, brown-eyed people could not have a blond, blue-eyed son, yet even so Elray was in the position of a parent. It was his duty to teach the essentials to the boy in his charge.

Jondelle said, shrewdly, "We could be attacked again. It would help if I knew how to defend myself. Please teach me how to use a knife."

"You expect to be attacked again?"

"I don't know. But if it did happen, then I want to be able to do as you did. Elray won't teach me. He doesn't like violence. He says that civilized people don't need to use it."

"He is right," said Dumarest flatly.

"But if a civilized man met one who wasn't?"

A question too shrewd for any young boy to ask . . . yet what was age when it came to understanding? At six, Dumarest had been hunting game with a crude sling, with hunger the penalty should he miss. At seven— He drew a deep breath, reluctant to remember.

"You hold a knife so." He demonstrated. "Thumb to the blade, the point held upward. Don't try to stab. You could miss or hit a bone or wedge it in some way and so disarm yourself. You use the edge to cut, so." He swept the blade through the air, turning it so that the late afternoon sun shone on the point and edge. "And if you have to defend yourself, never hesitate. Go in fast and do what has to be done. Don't be afraid of getting hurt, accept the fact that you may have to take a minor wound, and try not to be afraid. Fear will slow you down and give your opponent a chance to get you before you can get him. Aim for the eyes and then—"

"That will be enough!" Elray had approached unseen, his boots silent on the soft dirt. He stood, his thickset body tense with rage, his face mottled with anger. "Jondelle, go into the house!"

Dumarest watched him go, looked at the watching eyes of a cluster of workers, small men with lank hair and a subdued manner, their women peering from the windows of the shacks clustered around the house.

"You are our guest," said Elray tightly. "But even if you were my brother, I would never allow what I have just seen. What kind of man are you to teach a boy how to maim and kill? To use weapons of destruction? Is this how you repay my hospitality?"

Dumarest looked at the knife in his hand, the whiteness

of the knuckles, and the trembling of the point. Quickly he sheathed the blade.

"We owe you much," continued Elray. "I admit it. But some things I will not permit. Jondelle is a child and should be treated like one."

"He is a man," said Dumarest harshly. "A small one and young, but a man just the same. He will grow and meet others who did not have such squeamish guardians. If they think him soft, they will push and he will have no choice but to yield. He will lose his pride or, if he has it, will make a stand. And, dying, he will not thank you for the things you failed to teach."

He turned before the other could answer, striding quickly past the watching figures, heading for the distant ridge and the trees which laced the sky. Beyond lay more open ground, undulating plains unmarked by road or trail, the river a winding streak of pale emerald edged with clustered rushes. To the north mountains loomed, their summits capped with snow. A pastoral scene of peace and beauty, an oasis of tranquillity in which a man could sit and dream way his life. But beyond it, somewhere, lay the city and the field and the ships which would take him back into space and to other worlds. His world, perhaps . . . already he had lingered too long.

It was late when he returned, the sky a glitter of stars, of curtains of shimmering brilliance, of globes and clusters and sheets of glowing luminescence. The normal night-scene of any planet close to the heart of the galaxy, the Center where suns were close and world teemed in profusion.

Lights shone in the house and clustered shacks and the scent of cooking was heavy on the air. He heard voices as he passed through the main door, and paused at the sound of his name. Elray and the woman, he guessed, talking about the stranger they had taken into their home. He paused, listening.

"No!" Elray was firm. "I won't have it. Knives at his age. It's indecent!"

"Earl is a man who has lived hard. He has different values from your own." She paused and then added, softly, "If he hadn't, would you be sitting here now?"

"Are you reminding me again of what you choose to call my weakness?"

"It isn't weak to be gentle, Elray, but sometimes it can

be fatal. I want Jondelle to be strong. To stand on his own feet and to rely on nobody. Damn it, man! I want him to survive!"

Her cry came from the heart, the eternal cry of a mother afraid for her child. Dumarest felt its intensity, and so did Elray. When he next spoke, his voice was more subdued.

"I care for the boy, Makgar; you know that. It's as if he were my own. But what do we really know about Dumarest? A stranger. A traveler and perhaps more than that. The attack could have been planned, his intervention also. All of it designed to get him where he is at this very moment. And he is too close to Jondelle. The boy won't stay away from him, always he seems to be at his side, talking, listening, learning perhaps, or perhaps it is more than that. How can we be sure?"

"Three men dead, Elray. Dumarest badly wounded— that's how we can be sure. And—"

"Yes?"

"Their closeness worries you?"

"It does."

"And you can't guess the reason? Her voice held a tender note of understanding. "A traveler, you called him, a wanderer without a home or family to call his own. A man who, perhaps, yearns for a son. A boy to teach and train and make into an image of himself. I've watched them together and I know something of the loneliness he must feel. I had him under hypnotic sedation, don't forget, and in that condition there can be no deception. Dumarest is no enemy. He is a very lonely person who is looking for something. Searching for it. Perhaps, subconsciously, he may think that he has found it."

"The boy," said Elray thickly. "A surrogate son. And you? Are you eager to become his wife?"

Her amusement was genuine. "Elray? Are you jealous?"

"Can you deny it?"

"You're talking nonsense."

"You don't deny it," he said bleakly. "You can't, I've watched and I know."

Dumarest turned and moved softly through the door back into the star-shot night. He coughed, scuffed his boot, and slammed the panel hard against the wall as he reentered the house. Light shone through the open door of the room in which Elray and the woman sat at the table, bread, wine, the remains of a meal scattered before them.

Entering, he said, "It is time that I moved on. If you could give me a lift to the city, I would be grateful."

"You're leaving?" He caught the note of anguish in the woman's voice, saw the sudden look of relief in the man's eyes.

"Yes. There are things I have to do."

"But you aren't fit yet." Makgar rose to close fast the door and stood before him, the rise and fall of her breasts prominent beneath the fabric of her gown. "Your wound isn't wholly healed and you need more food and rest."

"I can get both in the city."

"I will be going there tomorrow," said Elray quickly. "You can ride with me."

"But——" With an effort she controlled herself. "I think you are being foolish," she continued flatly. "That is my opinion as a doctor. There is still the danger of complications from your wound. In five days I think you could walk to the city, but, at this time, to ride would be to take a foolish risk."

"There are doctors in the city," said Elray. "And the raft is stable. We will travel slow and in comfort." He added, "Stop fussing. Makgar. Earl is a grown man and knows what he wants to do."

"Yes," she said dully. "I supose that he does." Her eyes fell to the food on the table, lifted to meet Dumarest's level stare. "You haven't eaten," she accused. "We waited, but you didn't arrive and so——" Her hand made a little gesture. "At least you will eat before you go to your room?"

"Yes," he said. "I will eat."

CHAPTER
THREE

There were small sounds, the creak of timbers, the rustle of a leaf, the settling of boards and stairs. The starlight shone too brightly through the window and the air seemed to be filled with a restless urgency. Dumarest stirred, uneasy on the soft bed, instinct keeping him aware. He was leaving, a decision had been made, there was nothing more to do now but wait. Yet his uneasiness persisted and he could not sleep.

Rising, he crossed to the window and stared at the empty scene outside, the river a soft band of silver, the grass so dark as to be almost black. A few clouds drifted in the sky to the impact of a gentle wind. Softly he padded to the door and stood, listening. A murmur drifted to his ears as of voices wrapped and muffled and very distant. Dressing, he stepped outside the room and crept down the stairs. The murmur grew as he neared the door, strengthening as he opened it. A few lights shone in the clustered shacks and the sound grew louder. A chant, he realized, voices raised in muted harmony. A paean or an appeal—it was impossible to tell which. It rose and then died with shocking abruptness as a door opened to emit a flood of light. Framed in the opening Makgar stood, turned to face the interior from which came the thin, telltale cry of a newborn child.

"He will be well," she said to those within. "He will grow strong and tall and run like the wind. Your son will bring you joy."

The chant rose again as she closed the door and moved across the courtyard. She halted with a gasp as she saw Dumarest, one hand flying to her throat. She wore a robe loosely tied at the front, open at breast and thigh to reveal naked flesh. A thing quickly donned, he guessed, in order to answer an urgent summons.

"Earl! Is that you?"

"I heard the chant and came to see what caused it."

"A birth," she said. "There was some difficulty and they sent for me. A simple thing, but they are a simple people and cannot cope with the unexpected. Always they have to appeal to someone or something. Gods, spirits, even the wind and stars. Inbreeding has leeched all initiative out of their character, but they make good and docile workers."

"Where did you find them?"

"They've always been here, living in the woods and forests, primitive and riddled wih superstition. I suppose they must be the original people, though—" She broke off, staring at his face. "Is something wrong, Earl?"

"You called them the Original People."

"I meant those who were here first. Ourelle has been settled many times and there are all sorts of offshoot cultures. The planet is stable now, but there was a time when it was every man for himself and to hell with the consequences. You've seen Sargone? Of course you have . . . well, didn't you wonder why the streets are all curved? It was built by thieves and robbers who wanted a defense against line-of-sight weapons. At one time they levied tribute on every scrap of material entering or leaving the spacefield. Other fields were built, of course, and other patterns followed, but they have never really merged into a whole as they have done on other worlds. Sargone is the city-state, Relad the agricultural. To the west lies Frome and beyond it Ikinold. And then there is the sea-culture of Jelbtel." She made an impatient gesture. "This is no time or place for a history lesson, and I doubt if you are really interested."

"You would be wrong," he said. "I'm very interested. Particularly in the Original People."

"The Hegelt? That's what we call them. They are human but hopelessly superstitious and, as I said, inbred to the point of extinction. A cross would revitalize them, but they won't entertain the idea. No woman will give herself to a man not of her own people and no man will look for a foreign wife. My guess is that in a few more generations they will be either extinct or utterly degenerate. In the meantime they have their uses. Are you tired?"

"No."

"Then shall we walk a little? I won't be able to sleep now. Please?"

She took his hand and led him to a place beside the

river where the bank fell gently toward the rippling water. She first sat and then lay supine, one knee upraised so as to reveal the sweeping curve of her naked thigh. A posture of abandonment or of calculated seduction, or perhaps it was merely an attitude of total relaxation in the company of someone she could trust.

Dreamily she said, "Isn't it peaceful here? So very pleasant and calm. In time your life begins to adjust to the tempo of the elements and seasons. I think men make a mistake to cling to cities when they could live closer to nature."

"Nature isn't always kind," said Dumarest. He had sat beside her, facing the river, watching the ripple of the water. "What did you do before you married Elray?"

"I was a doctor."

"And?"

"A historian of sorts. I never really practiced medicine after I qualified. A chance was offered at the Kladour and I took it—biological investigation and gene structure of native life. That is why I know so much about the Hegelt. One of the professors had a theory, or had heard of a theory, that all men originated on the same world. Ridiculous, of course, but it was amusing to disprove it."

Dumarest said, "Did you?"

"Disprove it? Well, I didn't really have to. After all, the concept is fantastical nonsense. How could one planet provide all the people there are in the galaxy? And think of the different types." She stretched a little, careless of the way her robe fell from her shoulders. "Are you really interested in the Hegelt, Earl?"

"Not the Hegelt. The Original People."

"There is a difference?"

"The Original People are members of a religious cult whose basic tenet is that all mankind stemmed from a common source. They believe that source was a single planet which they call Terra. They are a secretive group who seek no converts and whose activities are shrouded in mystery. Have you ever heard of them? Is there any information about them in the Kladour?"

"To my knowledge, no."

"Can you be certain? In some old book, perhaps, a minor reference even. Anything."

She sensed the raw hunger in his voice, the hope, too

often thwarted, yet constantly alive. She lifted her shoulders from the sward, sitting with her hands clasped around her knees, looking at his profile, the hard line of the jaw stark in the glow from the sky.

Quietly she said, "There is nothing that I know of. But why are you so interested?"

"Terra is another name for Earth."

"Earth," she mused. "Once, in your delirium, you mentioned it. Earth. A place?"

"A world. My world."

"Could a planet have such a name?" Her voice was light, matching the tinkle of the water. "It's like calling a world sand or dirt or ground. This is earth." Her hand touched the soil. "But we call this place Ourelle."

"Earth is real," he insisted. "A world, old and scarred by ancient wars. The stars are few and there is a great, single moon which hangs like a pale sun in the night sky."

"A legend," she said. "I have heard of them. Worlds which have never existed. Jackpot and Bonanza, El Dorado, and Camelot. Eden too, though I think there is an actual planet called that."

"There are three," he said bleakly. "And there could be more. But there is only one Earth and I was born on its surface. One day I shall find it."

"But—" She broke off, frowning, and then said, carefully, as if talking to a child, "You were born on it, you say, and you must have left it. Then why can't you just go back to it?"

"Because no one knows where it is. It isn't listed in any almanac, the very name seems to have no meaning, the coordinates are missing. People think it is a legend and smile when I mention its name."

"A lost world," she said thoughtfully. "One on the edge of the galaxy; if the stars are few, it must be. There would be few ships and little trade. But you left it, you say?"

"As a boy. I stowed away on a ship and had more luck than I deserved. The captain was kind, an old man who regarded me as his son. He should have evicted me; instead he allowed me to work my passage. And then there were other journeys, other worlds."

Moving, always moving, and always toward the Center where planets were close and ships plentiful. Traveling for years until even the very name of Earth had been forgotten and it had become less than a dream. And the other years, the empty spaces, the constant search for someone, anyone, who would know the way back. The coordinates which would guide him home.

He felt the touch of her hand on his own and turned to face her, seeing her eyes, wide with sympathy, bright with emotion.

"I think I understand now," she said softly, "I knew you were searching for something and I thought—well, never mind. But I didn't guess—how could I have guessed? —that you were lost and searching for your home. Have you no clues? Nothing to guide you?"

Fragments. A sector of the galaxy, some notations, a name, other things. Enough to go on, if he could find the money to hire machines and experts, more to charter a vessel, still more to insure his survival. But, always, was the hope that he could find another way. A person who knew where Earth was to be found. Figures that would provide the answer.

"Earl!" Her fingers tightened on his hand and he sensed the heightening of her emotion. "Oh, Earl!"

Lightly he said, "There you have it, the story of my life. A runaway boy who thinks it's long past the time to go back home. Which is why I'm leaving tomorrow. Or is it today?"

She glanced at the stars and said, "Today. But must you go?"

"Yes."

"But why, Earl? You are welcome here. More than welcome."

"By Elray?"

"Of course! Surely you don't think that—" She broke off and then said, flatly, "You heard. You must have heard. You entered the house and then left to enter again. Well, what of it? What difference does it make?"

He made no answer, looking at the sky, at the silver thread of a metor reflected in the water of the river.

"We're married," she said dully. "On Ourelle such a contract is not all that important and can be broken any time either party wishes. But ours was never more than a marriage of convenience. My money paid for the farm and Elray was willing to work it. A mutual arrangement for mutual protection, because even on Ourelle a woman alone with a child finds life a little hard. And a boy needs a father,

a man to emulate, to follow, with whom to feel secure.
Earl!"

"No!"

"Jondelle likes you. He needs you. The farm is mine.
If—"

"No," he said again, harshly. "Forget it!"

She knew better than to argue, leaning back instead
to sprawl on the scented grass, the starlight warm on the
soft contours of thigh and shoulders, the rich swell of
her breasts. Tempting bait for a lonely man, more so when
coupled with the farm and the security it offered, harder
still to resist when there was a boy who had already won
more than his friendship. A child he could so easily
regard as his son. A good exchange for the bleak empti-
ness between the stars, the endless quest for a forgotten
world.

Quietly she said, "This is what could happen, Earl. We
could all go into the city, the divorce arranged, the
marrage performed, provision made for Elray. You would
rule here and you could watch Jondelle grow, teach him
the things he should know and guide him on the path he
must take. But you don't want that. So instead I'll make
you a proposition. Stay here for a while. Guard the boy.
Give him a year of your life."

A determined woman, he thought, and a clever one. In
a year he would be trapped, unwilling or unable to leave
the boy, ready to fall into a new arrangement. And it would
not take a year—not with her pushing and Elray aiding by
his own sullen aggression.

"Earl?"

"It's getting late. We had better get back to the house."

"Aren't you interested?"

"No."

"Not even for the boy's sake?"

"If you're afraid for the lad, then sell your farm and
move into the city. Hire guards and watchers. Better still,
take ship and hide on some other world."

"As you have done, Earl?"

He caught the inflection and remembered that she
had held him beneath her hypnotic influence, helpless to
resist any investigation she had cared to make. And a curious woman would not have stopped at merely discovering
his name.

"As I have done," he admitted. "But you know that."

"I guessed. I didn't pry, you have my word for that, but some things are obvious. A fear you try to hide, a thing you must keep secret and—" She broke off, looking at the sky. Earl!"

"What is it?"

"There! See?"

A patch of darkness against the splendor of the sky. An oblong which moved and grew even as they watched, to settle beyond the house and the cluster of shacks.

"A raft," he said. "Visitors, perhaps?"

A roar gave the answer. The crash of explosives followed by a pillar of flame, repeated as the workers screamed and ran into the sheltering darkness. More flame rising to paint the area red and orange, leaping tongues feeding on walls and roofs, filling the air with smoke and the stink of char.

Dumarest felt the woman leave his side and race toward the house. He followed her, caught an arm, flung her to the ground, one hand clamped over her mouth.

"Be silent," he hissed into her ear. "You promise?"

She nodded, gulping as he released her mouth, sobbing as she looked at the devastation.

"The boy, Earl! Dear God, the boy!"

He was in the house together with Elray and a handful of servants and, as yet, the house was untouched. Dumarest narrowed his eyes as he stared at the mounting glare. Against the burning shacks he could see bizarre shapes, men with protective armor pointed and fluted in spiked curves, heads masked and helmeted with plumes and ribbons. Madmen hell-bent on wanton destruction—or men who wanted to give that exact impression.

He watched as one lifted an arm and hurled an object into a barn. Thunder, smoke, and flame gushed from the open door. Others ran over the courtyard, lances thrusting at cringing shapes, keening laughter rising above the dying screams.

"Melevganians," said the woman. "From the lands beyond the deserts to the south. Madmen the lot of them. Earl! We must save the boy!"

He held her close to the dirt, one hand hard against her back, feeling the bunch and jerk of muscle as she tried to rise.

"We can do nothing," he snapped. "Not yet. And the boy is in no immediate danger." He stared at the house.

The windows showed no lights, the glass ruby with reflected firelight, and that was wrong. There were no internal lights —but it wasn't that—what was wrong was that no window had yet been opened. Elray must surely be awake, the servants too, and there would be arms, lasers perhaps, missile weapons which could kill an injured beast if nothing else. And a gun which could kill an animal could just as easily kill a man. Elray now should be behind an open window ready to defend his own.

He looked again at the attackers. A dozen, he guessed, at least ten, but it was hard to tell in the dancing firelight. They moved in sudden darts, stabbing, moving on, grotesque in their helmets and armor. A raiding party intent on easy destruction and wary of approaching the house and the danger it could contain—or a group eliminating opposition with calculated precision?

He said, "Are you sure of what they are?"

Again he felt her strain beneath his hand, then relax, sobbing.

Deliberately he slapped her cheek with his free hand. "Control yourself! Answer me: are you certain?"

"The way they're dressed," she said. "The way they are acting. Lunatics, insane, drugged and degenerate, and having fun. They will burn and destroy and kill everything alive. Everything, Earl! Everything!"

"Why isn't Elray shooting them down? Are there no weapons in the house?"

"A couple of rifles, but he won't use them. He hates violence." Her voice hardened. "The damn coward! If he lives through this, I'll tear out his throat! Earl, what can we do?"

A dozen men armed with grenades, lances, and probably missile weapons. Protected by helmets and armor and drunk on blood-lust. And against them he had only a knife.

He said, "Move toward the back of the house. Be careful; drop if you see anything and freeze until it's gone. Get inside if you can and get the boy. A rifle too, if you can manage. Then get back outside and head for the river. Follow it to the crest and hide among the trees. If anyone tries to stop you, shoot without hesitation. Shoot, then run."

"And you, Earl?"

"I'll attack from the other side and try to create a

diversion." He saw a gout of flame rimmed with flying sparks burst from a point close to the house. Against it armored figures began to move with grim purpose toward the untouched building. "Move!"

He rose as she slipped away, crouched, running in a wide circle so as to hug the edge of the firelight. A dark shape raced toward him, one of the workers breaking free, whimpering in terror, an armored figure close behind. As Dumarest watched, the lanced lifted, aimed, spat a tongue of fire. The worker exploded in a gout of flame.

Lasers would have been silent and more efficient but to madmen, reveling in the sound and fury of destruction, less satisfying. The lance was a double-duty weapon, a sharp point and a missile launcher of some kind built into the shaft. Dumarest sprang to one side as it leveled toward him, sprang again as fire jetted from the tip, a third time as flame and noise blasted from where he had stood. Then he was within the length of the weapon, left hand sweeping it aside, right foot lashing out in a savage kick to an armored knee.

He felt something yield and heard the figure scream with maniacal rage. A fist lifted, clenched, and swept down like a mace, firelight glinting from the spikes set on each knuckle. Wind brushed his cheek as he dodged and before the fist could strike again he was behind the armored figure, left hand clamped around the throat, the knife in his right scraping as he thrust it through the vision slit in the helmet. Twice he stabbed, blinding, killing, rending the brain, tearing free the steel as the figure collapsed.

Quickly Dumarest searched the body. A pouch held three round objects, grenades, simple things with a pin and safety catch. He thrust them into a pocket of his tunic. The lance was long, clumsy, a button set close to the end of the shaft. He looked toward the house. Three figures were close to the door, one almost touching the panel, the others a little toward the rear and to one side. Still more, apparently tired of ravaging the shacks, moved to join them.

The dead man made a convenient rest. Dumarest sprawled behind him, the lance resting on the armored chest, his eyes narrowed as he stared along the shaft. The weapon probably fired a rocket of some kind and he doubted if it would be too accurate. The light was bad, the shadows deceptive, and if he missed the figure close to the door he could well blow in the panel. He moved the tip a little, steadied his aim, and pressed the button.

Fire blossomed from the wall of the house high and to one side of the little group. Adjusting his aim, he fired again, twice more, then the weapon was empty. Before the house a man staggered, shrieking, beating at the fire which wreathed his helmet. Two others lay in twitching heaps, a third crawled like a broken insect over the dirt. As Dumarest watched, he rose, staggering, shaking his head: semi-stunned by concussion but otherwise unhurt.

Four down but there were others and the woman had to be given her chance. Dumarest stood upright, a grenade in his hand. He drew the pin and threw it toward the house, turning before it fell, running as it exploded, his figure clear against the light from the burning shacks. Somewhere beyond the fires would be their raft, probably unattended or, if guarded, watched by restless and impatient men. To those who had seen him it would be important—they would want to save it from damage, and they would follow.

Almost too late he saw the twin figures with raised lances, ribbons bright on crested helmets, firelight warm on points and flutes of armor. They stood at the end of the open ground, blocking his path, others running from the rear to trap him between. Without hesitation he lunged to one side, hit the burning wall of a shack, rolled through fire, holding his breath, eyes tight-closed, feeling the kiss of flame on his hands and face, hearing the crisp of his hair. The shack was small; momentum carried him to and through the opposite wall to roll in a shower of sparks on the ground beyond. Rising, he threw a second grenade, running before it exploded, hearing the roar, the screams, and shouts of command.

And another scream, high, shrill, coming from the back of the house.

CHAPTER

FOUR

Makgar had been taken. She stood, an armored figure holding each arm, very pale in the starlight. The house shielded the little group from the light of the fires, the shadow accentuating the darkness so that for a moment Dumarest couldn't see the third man. Then he moved and the light shone on yellow hair—the boy caught in his arms.

"Please," she begged. "Don't take the boy. Let him go. I'll give you anything you want, but let him go."

One of the men holding her tittered, his voice thin and high, crazed and ugly.

"What can you give, woman, that we do not already have?"

"Money. I'll sell the farm and give you what I get. More. I'll work and you can have that too. I'll be your slave if you want—but don't hurt the boy."

"A fine child," said the one who had spoken. "A strong child. A young one who can be—manipulated. Clamps and cramps and bindings to guide his growth. Racks and weights and implements to alter and stretch and turn him into a thing of joy. Have you seen our menagerie? Some of our specimens you would never take for men."

He laughed, the sound like the rasp of a nail on slate, a degraded keening devoid of amusement.

"No!" Sweat shone on her face and her eyes were wild. "Not that! Dear God, not that!"

"The prospect amuses you, woman? After all, why should he be as other men? An ordinary person when he could be fashioned to become a thing unique. The arms, for example, lengthened to twice what they would normally be. The legs too, the head shaped into a cone, the back guided into a serpentine curve. It amuses you to think of it?"

The man holding the boy said, "Enough."

"You object?"

"There will be no more such talk." His voice was deep, reverberating from the closed helmet. "We have the boy and now we can leave."

"So soon? When there is sport yet to be had? I think not." The thin voice held a menacing snarl. "The house still stands, the woman lives, and there is another. He too must be taken care of before the dawn."

"Do as you wish, but the boy must not be harmed. Attend me to the raft."

He stepped forward, confident of being obeyed, his figure huge as he stepped into the light from the burning shacks. Behind him the woman strained against the metal-clad hands which gripped her.

"Jondelle!"

The boy gave no answer. He seemed to be asleep in the big man's arms, his head lolling against the armored shoulder. Drugged, thought Dumarest, certainly not dead. They would have taken less trouble with a dead boy, and the lad was not that. He caught the movement of the lifting chest, the beads accentuating the slight inhalation, bright colors shifting beneath the light. On the pale cheeks the lashes looked like delicate lace.

The big man halted. "Come," he boomed. "Attend me. I shall not ask again."

The thin voice tittered, "You ask? Not order?"

"I ask."

"Then we shall accommodate you. We are reasonable men, most reasonable, but we do not take kindly to orders. And, as we walk, I shall think of how to amuse this woman. A fire at her feet, perhaps, not too hot or too large, but just enough to shorten her height. And then—well, such things must not be hurried. I shall dwell on it as we walk at your back."

As they passed, Dumarest rose like a ghost behind them. Helmets limited vision; they could see ahead but not to either side and certainly not where he followed. And there were no others at the rear of the house; he had made certain of that. But he would have to act fast before they met their companions.

Three men. The one holding the boy would be hampered, slow to turn, slower to act. The ones holding the woman were more dangerous, to beat them would need speed and accuracy, but if he could free her he would have an ally.

If she could forget her concern for the boy, resist her natural impulse to run toward him, and take advantage of her opportunity.

Stepping forward, he tripped up the man to her right. It was a thing quickly and easily done. One foot caught on his instep and lifted so as to catch behind the other. He toppled, dropping his lance, releasing his hold on the woman in order to save himself. As he fell, Dumarest lunged forward, gripped the other man's right shoulder, and jerked the trapped arm hard against his body. He felt the snap of bone as the elbow yielded beneath the armor and snapped at the woman as the hand fell from her arm.

"The other one. Take him!"

He snatched the knife from his boot as a spiked fist drove toward his face, feeling the rip as the cruel points tore at his scalp. The blade lifted and lanced at the helmet, seeking a slit and finding only perforations. Again the left fist came toward him like a club, catching his shoulder, ripping at the plastic to reveal the glint of metal beneath. Before it could lift again, Dumarest had swung up his left arm, lifting the visor and exposing the face beneath. It was painted, snarling, a vicious mask of animal ferocity. The mouth gaped to show filed teeth, closed to send them clashing against the steel of the blade. Dumarest jerked it free, thrust again at the glaring eyes, sending the point between the ball and the bony ridge of the eyebrow, driving it deep into the brain.

From behind came a frenzied screaming.

Makgar had taken her chance. The fallen man had tried to rise and she had jumped on his back, sending him to the dirt, her hands lifting his visor and busying themselves beneath. She raised them, red with blood, naked breasts heaving beneath the parted robe.

"He isn't dead," she panted. "But he can't see. I got his eyes. The boy?"

The big man had gone, the boy with him. Dumarest snatched up a lance and ran past the burning shacks. A dark figure came from one side, arms empty, a lance raised. Dumarest fired, thumbing the button, sending a stream of missiles toward him. One hit the ground at his feet, another slammed into the armored chest. The third was wasted.

"Jondelle," she said. "Quick!"

The fires fell behind, lapping at a wall of star-shot night. The contrast was too great; against the firelight all was darkness and illusive shadows. Dumarest halted, conscious of the danger, the fires at his back, and enemies waiting. The woman threw aside all caution.

"Quick!" she gasped. "Hurry!"

Somewhere was the raft and one man, more likely several. The big man with the boy and the others who must have been left on guard. Dumarest hit the woman, throwing the weight of his body against her flank, and sending her sprawling on the ground. He followed, holding her down as streaks of fire passed overhead to explode among the burning shacks.

"Earl!"

"Be silent!"

Sound could betray their position. He lifted his head cautiously, staring at the glittering sky. Against it something moved, dark, regular in shape, and slowly rising.

"The raft! Earl, they're getting away!"

She rolled from beneath his hand, rising before he could stop her, running over the grass toward the ascending vehicle. He reared upright, snatching out the last grenade, then throwing it aside as useless. He could throw it and maybe send it to explode in the body of the raft, but that would certainly kill the boy. But he could damage it perhaps, slow it in some way, maybe even bring it down. He lifted the lance, aimed, and touched the button.

Fire exploded against metal, a brilliant gush which showed the underside of the raft, the helmeted heads peering over the edge. Two of them. There would be another, the pilot, and maybe yet one more, that of the big man who held the boy. He fired again, the missile hitting the back edge, the light revealing the shafts pointing toward him. He fired twice more, guessing where the engine would be, the generator of the current which fed the anti-gravity units of the raft.

And then the lance was exhausted and he had thrown it aside, falling to hug the ground, covering his ears as the return fire blazed around him.

Miraculously he was unhit, rising as the missiles ceased, conscious of the ache caused by bruising fragments, a trickle of blood running over his face from a minor wound.

"Makgar!" He looked around, wiping blood from his eyes. "Makgar?"

She lay looking very small and fragile in the torn ruin of her robe, the bright fabric brighter than before with the ruby of her blood. Around her the soil was pitted with jagged craters, the dirt burned and tormented, wet where she lay. The distant firelight caught her eyes, enhancing their brightness, their pain.

"Earl?"

"They got away," he said flatly. "I think I damaged the raft so they couldn't move fast or far. And you?"

"My side. It was like being kicked. Earl—"

"Don't talk," he said. "Don't do anything. Just lie there until I return."

"You're going?"

"They left in a hurry," he said grimly. "Some of them may have been left behind. I want to make sure."

The area was lifeless, silent aside from the rustle of flame. Close to the house Dumarest heard the keening of the man Makgar had injured, but ignored him, moving to the back and an opened window, slipping inside with knife ready and eyes strained. The workers were dead, the servants huddled where they had run to Elray for protection. He lay beside a rifle, the side of his head a crushed mess, one hand outstretched as if in mute appeal. Perhaps he had tried to do that, talk instead of act, beg instead of using the rifle which could have saved his life. Dumarest picked it up, a good weapon, fully loaded, the missiles capable of penetrating any armor ever worn. Elray could have climbed to an upper room, picked off the invaders as they stood before the fires, shot them down as they tried to climb the stairs. Had he acted, the boy would be safe and the woman unharmed.

She looked at him as he stooped over her.

"Earl?"

"It's all right," he said. "I'm going to take you into the house."

"Elray?"

"Dead."

"I'm glad," she whispered. "He could have done something, used one of the guns, anything. He didn't have to let them take the boy."

"Maybe he didn't."

"They were waiting," she said. "In the house. They

grabbed me as I—well, never mind. That isn't important now. But he could have done something. He promised to look after the boy. He promised that."

She groaned as he lifted her, blood welling from the torn wound in her side, dark, turgid.

"It hurts," she whispered. "God, how it hurts!"

Her head lolled as he carried her into the house, her eyes blank, glazed with pain. He snapped on every light he could find, found her room, stripped off the bed covers and laid her on the sheet. Flinging the robe into a corner, he studied her naked body. The missile had hit her side, exploding, creating intense pressures, and causing havoc to the internal organs. He found warm water and washed the wound free of dirt and fiber, using clean sheets to bind it close, fretting out the material before applying it so as to promote coagulation. In a cabinet downstairs he found medical supplies and studied them, frowning. Quick-time would have helped, slowing the metabolism so as to make a day seem but a few minutes, but there was little need for it outside the ships which traversed space—the passengers who rode High using it to shorten the tedium of the journey.

He found antibiotics and a hypogun, loading the instrument and testing it against a sheet of paper, the air blast driving the drug through the material as it would skin and fat. Another vial contained a sedative, a third a means to kill pain. He carried them upstairs and injected them all.

"Earl." The drugs were quick-acting; incredibly she managed to smile. "You're efficient, Earl. I like that in a man. You know what to do and you do it without hesitation, but you shouldn't waste your time."

"It's my time."

"And my life—what there is of it."

"You're hurt," he said flatly. "Badly, but you're still alive. If you want to, you can stay that way. Give up and I might as well bury you now."

"I'm a doctor," she said. "You don't have to lie to me."

"Am I lying?"

"No, but—" She caught herself, forcing open her eyes. "I feel so sleepy and I mustn't sleep. There is something. The boy. Earl!"

"He'll be all right. The man who took him won't

let him come to harm. And we'll find him. I promise that."

She stirred, fighting the drugs he had blasted into her bloodstream.

Quickly he said, "Have you a radio? Some means of summoning aid?"

"No, no radio, we wanted to be isolated. Just—"

"Sleep now," he said.

"I mustn't." Again she dragged herself awake. "You shouldn't have given me that sedative. There are things I have to say."

"Later."

"Now, before it's too late. You've got to promise me . . . Earl . . . you must . . . "

She sighed and yielded to the drugs, relaxing and looking younger than he had ever seen her before. And yet she was far from being a girl, the lines of her body held a lush maturity, the muscles firm, the fat giving a soft roundness. He covered her, piling on soft quilts, arranging her pillow, and then, mouth cruel, he left the house and went into the courtyard.

The man she had blinded was still alive. He crawled in his armor like a stricken monster, keening, his spiked gloves scrabbling at the dirt. Dumarest watched him without pity, remembering the things he had said, the threats he had made. Catching a shoulder, he spun the man over onto his back, the ruined face ugly with its paint in the fading light of the fires.

"Listen to me," said Dumarest. "I want to tell you something amusing. You are blind and can't see, but I will describe it to you. A new formation of a man. A fire to char away his feet, a knife to remove his hands, his ears, his nose. The same knife to slit his tongue and to release the intestines from his stomach. Acid to burn a pattern on his flesh. You appreciate the image? A work .of art suitable for inclusion in your menagerie. You will be that man, unless you talk."

The thin lips parted to show the filed teeth.

"My eyes! The pain—"

"Will get a damn sight worse if you don't tell me what I want to know! Who are you? Where are you from?"

"They lied!" The voice was a fretful whine. "They said there would be no opposition. Just a few Hegelt, a woman and a boy."

"Who lied?"

"Those who wanted to come with us. For amusement, they said. Money and a raft and we could do as we pleased. A raid, that was all. A night of fun. My eyes!"

"The man who took the boy. What is his name?"

"Why should I care?"

"Where did he come from?"

"What are strangers to us?"

"Damn you!" snarled Dumarest. "Talk!"

Incredibly the creature smiled. "I will talk. I am Tars Krandle, a noble of Melevgan, and if you will take me to where I can receive medical aid I will reward you well. Your own weight in silver, women of chosen attractiveness, a selection from my private—" He broke off, laughing, the thin sound echoing madness. "Or I will sing you the dirge of the Emphali. They sing when they are being slowly torn apart—did you know that? I have a most entertaining recording and will give you a copy, if you will only aid me. Or—" He tittered. "Or perhaps I won't talk at all. You can't make me. No one can force a member of my race to do anything they choose not to do. Not you, not anyone. We are the elect."

"You will talk." Dumarest rasped the knife from his boot and rested the flat of the blade against the flaccid cheek. "Feel that? It's a knife. I'm going to make it red-hot and then I'll touch you again. Need I tell you where?"

"You will not make me talk. No one can tell a noble of Melevgan what to do. We know how to live—and we know when to die."

"You will die," promised Dumarest savagely. "But you will take a long time and the waiting will not be pleasant. Feel the heat of the fires? They are close and could be closer. Now tell me who the man was and why he wanted the boy."

"I don't know. What are such things to me?"

"Where was he taking him?"

Dumarest jerked back as the man surged upward in a sudden explosion of energy, sensing rather than seeing the gloved hands rising, the spikes turned inward toward his head. Easily he avoided them, watching as they clashed together, to fall and beat at the armored chest, the protected groin. Screaming with maniacal rage, the Melevganian rose, his fists beating at the air, the open front of his helmet. Blood shone redly on the spikes as, still screaming, he staggered blindly into a glowing mound of ash, to fall, still shrieking, into the heart of the red-hot embers.

Bleakly Dumarest watched him burn. The man had created havoc, killed without compunction, and threatened horrors all for his own amusement. An insane monster who had chosen the manner of his own death—and who had died taking his knowledge with him.

He stretched, conscious of the ache in his body, the sting of the burns on hands and face, but there were things to be done before he could apply medications. The shacks had burned, the entire area a shambles, the dead lying with blank faces toward the sky. Dumarest let them lie. Beneath the helmets the faces of the armored men were the same as those he had already seen. The strangers, whoever they were, had all escaped in the raft. Two of them at least, he guessed. The big man would never have trusted the vehicle to the blood-crazed insanity of the Melevganians even if they had been willing to forego their amusement. But there had been another raft, Elray's, and he had to find it.

It was buried beneath a mound of splintered wood and stone, the metal bent, the engine damaged by fragments. He cleared it, working until the rising sun threw a pale green light over the area and his head swam with fatigue. And, with the dawn, came furtive shapes, the Hegelt returning to keen over their dead, their voices rising to blend with the morning breeze.

CHAPTER

FIVE

The room was as he remembered, warm, soft with golden light, the air scented with pungent aromas. At his desk Akon Batik wore the same robe of black and yellow, the jewel in his cap a living, ruby eye. He poured wine and said, after the first sip, "A sad story. A tragedy. But on Ourelle such things happen. On other worlds too, I have no doubt. But why have you come to me?"

"For help," said Dumarest. "For information."

"Which you think I can provide?"

"Which I think you may be able to obtain. A boy was stolen. A young lad who lived quietly on a farm. I want to know why."

Akon Batik shrugged, thin shoulders rising beneath his robe. "For ransom, perhaps? That is the obvious answer. For the whim of someone who had seen the boy and desired what they saw? For revenge against the mother? As a means to force others to obey their will? As a toy, a pet, or someone to train along a selected path? And what is it to you? A boy . . . there are millions of boys. One more or less—what does it matter?"

"It matters," said Dumarest. "To me."

"But not to me. You can appreciate that?"

A man of business who concerned himself only with profit and loss. On this and other worlds a man of sense and logic who took care of his own and remained clear of personal involvement. Dumarest sipped at his wine, not tasting the lambent fluid, knowing that he had to deal with the other on his own terms.

"You know the city," he said quietly. "You would be able to discover if men were hired to do a certain thing. You might even be able to find out who had hired them."

"Perhaps."

"I have money, as you know. I would be willing to pay for whatever help you could give."

The jeweler pursed his lips. "A business proposition? You present the matter in a more attractive light. But you said the raiders were Melevganians."

"There were others with them. Not Melevganians and maybe from the city. And certainly it was men from the city who tried to take the boy at first."

"Three men," said Akon Batik softly. "Yes, I heard of how they were found, but they were strangers." He paused, then added. "Perhaps it would have been best had you let them have their way."

A farm ruined, men and women slaughtered like beasts, and still the boy had been taken. Dumarest looked at his goblet, the tension of his hand.

"No," he said. "I couldn't do that."

"In any case, the thing is done and no man can reverse the passage of time. But I must warn you, those who took the boy are obviously strong. They will not be gentle should they find you an embarrassment. And, to be honest, I cannot understand your concern. He is not your son. You owe his family no allegiance. No one, as yet, has paid you to find him. Why are you willing to risk your life?"

"I gave my word."

"And, for you, that is enough." Akon Batik sipped thoughtfully at his wine. "I am not a sentimental man, but I can appreciate the strength of a promise given. Very well, I will do what I can. Be at the House of the Gong tonight and I will send a man to tell you what I have found. You will give him ten stergals."

"And for yourself?"

"You will give fifty to the man at the gate. You wish more wine?"

"Thank you, no."

"Then may good fortune attend you."

"And may happiness fill your days."

A cab took Dumarest to the Kladour and he stood looking up at the vast bulk of the building. The sun caught the fluted spire, the gilded ball on the summit, turning it into an eye-bright point of flame. Inside it was cool, wide halls sending soft echoes from the vaulted ceiling. A receptionist, a young girl, her face dusted with lavender, her eyes bright with inset flakes of reflective material, stared with frank admiration at his lean figure, curious as she noted his burned skin and singed hair.

"Could I help you, sir?"

"Yes. I have a problem. I am trying to find a man, a professor who works here or who used to work here. I don't know his name, but he once had a woman assistant. Makgar. He field was biological investigation and gene structure of native life. Can you help me?"

"No," she said reluctantly. "I'm sorry, I can't."

"But surely there would be records. It was a few years ago, I admit, but possibly someone would remember."

"Your interest?"

"I am making an investigation into the divergencies of various races from a common norm. I heard that the professor would have valuable information, and it is barely possible that I could help him in his own inquiries. If you could check with your personnel department?"

Professor Ashlen was well past middle age, with a balding scalp and muscles which had long since run to fat. He sat in an office musty with old files wearing a stained smock over a shirt of maroon and gray. He rose as Dumarest entered and held out his hand.

"You take it," he said. "You shake it and then let it go. It's an old custom."

"Yes," said Dumarest. "I know." The touch of the palm was moist, clammy.

"So few people do," said Ashlen. He sat and waved his visitor to a chair. "It's a little test of my own. If someone comes claiming to be an investigator of the human race, I assume that he has studied many cultures. If he has, then he would know why I put out my hand."

"You told me what to do," reminded Dumarest.

"So I did. That was careless of me. Now tell me: how did such a custom originate in the first place?"

"As a means of proving peaceful intention. I show you my bare hand and you touch it with your own. Naked hands can hold no weapons."

"And the other one? The left hand which is not extended?"

"Perhaps that held a knife behind the back," said Dumarest dryly. "Just in case. Do you remember a woman who used to work with you? Makgar. Tall, dark, well-built. A few years ago now."

"Makgar?" Ashlen frowned. "Is that what you came to talk about? I understood that you were interested in divergent races."

"I am, and the theory that all life originated on one world. But—"

"That is nonsense," said the professor firmly. "It is an attractive theory and one which rises from time to time, but, believe me, it has no foundation of truth. Men evolved on a variety of worlds much at the same time. There has been movement, of course, new worlds colonized and settlements founded, but to seriously consider that all men came from one small world is ludicrous. In fact, I proved it to be a complete fallacy."

"You and Makgar?"

"Makgar? Well, yes, she helped on the routine side, but I can fairly claim the credit for exposing the illogic of the contention. Of course, I can understand how such a notion could arise. Take Ourelle, for example. You are a stranger here?"

Dumarest nodded.

"A most peculiar world." Ashlen produced a map and unrolled it on his cluttered desk. "Here is the city of Sargone where we are now." His fingers rapped a patch of yellow. Here the plains of Relad where the majority of the Hegelt are to be found. Then here we have the Valley of Charne where there is a most peculiar race of yellow-skinned people. Note, the Hegelt are dark brown and the Charnians yellow. You see the implication?"

"Two races on one world," said Dumarest.

"Not so. The Hegelt are the original people and the Charnians the result of a later colonization. Then, to the north, we have the Shindara. And there are Frome and Ikinold and others. I won't bore you with their names. The point is they are all different in skin color, facial characteristics, and even physical peculiarities. It is natural to assume that if such variety could be found on one world, then they could have coexisted together in the past. On the mythical world from which legend has it they all orginated."

"Earth?"

"You have heard the name?" Ashlen shrugged. "But then, as an investigator into the divergencies of race, you would. A part of the legend, of course. My own conclusion is that it is another name for Eden which, as you must know, was the name of the original paradise. Another legend born of the tribulations of the early settlers when times were hard. They consoled themselves with talk of fabulous places and a world on which no man had to work and everything was provided by some race of beneficent creatures called, I think, angels. However, as I was saying, the existence of many races on Ourelle does not prove that all the races in the galaxy could have at one time shared one planet. In fact, the reverse is true, because we know they came here in various waves of colonization. Small groups which remained apart and still do. Societies and cultures which have found a stability and a certain harmony."

Dumarest said, "Harmony? The Melevganians?"

"Perhaps I should have said stability, but the Melevganians—" Ashlen shook his head. "They are insane and I mean that in a literal sense. Their gene structure has been altered due to the mutation-inducing radiations of the area in which they live. Their sense of values has little if nothing to do with what we regard as the norm. They are willful, caring nothing for anything but their most immediate desire. Unpredictable, dangerous, and yet fascinating to any student of the human species."

"I saw one die once," said Dumarest. "He threw himself into a fire."

"Faced with an impossible situation they will seek self-destruction," said the professor. "A maniacal hate which turns against themselves at what they regard as a failure to master their immediate environment. And they have an infinite capacity for revenge. They reside here." His finger tapped the map. "A sunken area surrounded by high mountains. With rafts they could escape, but they have a limited technology and, fortunately for the rest of Ourelle, a disinclination to leave their own territorial area. They make raids at times, disgusting affairs, but mostly they are contained by the peoples in adjoining areas."

Dumarest said, thoughtfully, "But they have contact with the outside. They trade?"

"Yes. As I said, they have a limited technology and are unable to produce much of what they use. However, they do find gems and heavy metals in the mountains which surround them. There are rumors that they have slaves to work the mines, but no one knows for certain. My personal opinion is that they do. Their arrogance would not allow them to perform menial tasks."

Ashlen reached for a thick pile of graphs. "And now let me show you the result of my investigations. You will see that, based on a cross-section of a thousand samples, there is a distinct . . ."

Dumarest let him ramble on, sitting back in a wooden chair, his eyes thoughtful as he stared at the emerald patch of the window. A girl brought them cups of tisane and he drank the tangy liquid more from politeness than from any reason of thirst. Around him the Kladour hummed with quiet efficiency, the repository of knowledge on this world, the pride of the city. And yet it contained nothing he did not already know about the planet he sought, and he could tell the professor nothing he would be willing to accept. His mind was closed, his eyes blinded to the possibility that he could be wrong. He was science and science had spoken and the world on which Dumarest had been born to him simply did not and could not exist.

A familiar reaction and another hope frustrated, but he had come for more than information about Earth.

"The woman," he said as the professor paused. "Makgar. Tell me about her."

"A woman. A good assistant. What more can I say?"

"Did she have a child? A son?"

"I believe so." Ashlen frowned. "Yes, now that I come to think of it, she did."

"How did she get her position here?"

"How do I know? These things are done by personnel. I wanted an assistant and they found me one. She seemed to know her job."

Short answers of little value. Dumarest restrained his impatience. "Did she talk to you at all about her past? Was she born here? Do you know her home world?"

"She claimed to be a doctor. She could have been, it was unimportant and unessential to her duties. I don't think she was born on Ourelle. Something she said once about the light. She mentioned a place called Veido, it was in casual conversation, and she seemed to have made a slip of the tongue. That's why I remember it."

"Try to remember something else," urged Dumarest. "Has anyone, at any time, ever asked about her?"

"No."

"Why did she leave?"

"Really!" Ashlen blew out his cheeks, his eyes hard with anger. "I entertained you because I took you for a colleague, but you seem to be more interested in the woman than my work. She left, I think, to leave the city. I simply didn't take that much interest." He touched a button on his desk. "And now, if you will excuse me? The usher will show you out."

"A moment." Dumarest rose and stood, tall and somber at the edge of the desk. Looking down at the professor, he said, "One more question—and this time think about it. Did she, at any time, mention the father of her child?"

"I—"

"Think about it, man! Did she?"

Ashlen swallowed. "No, she didn't. Not once. I assumed that he was dead, if I bothered to think about it at all. But why ask me all these things? Why don't you ask her?"

"I can't," said Dumarest harshly. "She's dead."

CHAPTER

SIX

She had died in the afternoon when the sun was high and casting a delicate patina over her hair. She had lain in the body of the raft, cushioned by quilts and blankets, more covering her from feet to chin. She had been restless, febrile, with an ooze of blood seeping from between her lips. And Dumarest, haggard from days without sleep, had been unable to save her.

It had taken too long to repair the raft and the Hegelt had been useless. Numbed by their losses, they could only sit and mourn their dead. Even when repaired the craft was slow, drifting over the ground like a windblown feather, demanding constant attention to keep it aloft and on course. He had been forced to land many times to work on the engine, more to bathe her fevered cheeks and wipe the crusted blood from her mouth. She had tried to remain conscious, refusing more sedatives, knowing she rode with death at her side.

"I'm dying, Earl. Don't argue with me, I know."

"We are all dying, Makgar."

"Then I'm ahead of my time." Her hands moved, checking her body. "The spleen is ruined, the pancreas also. The intestines are in a mess and both stomach and lungs are perforated." She tried to smile. "I'm not in what you'd call very good condition."

"We'll make it."

"In this wreck? God knows how you ever got it going in the first place. You could almost walk as fast. And how much longer can you go without sleep?"

"As long as I have to. And you're going to keep going as long as you have to. Until we can get you to a hospital."

"To life-support mechanisms, regrafts and regrowths, slow-time and all the rest of it. It's already too late, Earl. I'd be dead now, if it wasn't for you. Earl!"

He caught her hand and felt the pressure of her fingers as she fought the pain.

Bitterly he said, "Where did you hide your medicines? The drugs we could have used. You had to have more than what I found."

"In the shack, Earl. The one in which the baby was born. I left my bag there, I didn't need it, and there was no need to take it. The baby," she said. "Dear God, how can things shaped like men be so vile? The baby—and my boy. Jondelle!"

He saw the agony on her face and tore his hand free, lifting the hypogun and blasting pain-killers into her blood.

"No!" She shook her head as he adjusted the instrument. "I don't want to sleep. I can't. The boy—"

"I'll find him, Makgar."

"You promise that? Earl, you promise?"

"I promise."

"He's so small, so young and helpless. I can't bear to think of him in the hands of those beasts. You've got to save him, Earl."

"I will. I give you my word."

A promise to ease the hurt of a dying woman, but one he would keep. She sighed and seemed to relax, her eyes closing.

"Earl," she murmured. "I love you. I've loved you from the first. Elray was right. I wanted you, not him. I told you that. You should have agreed."

It would have made no difference. Leaning close, he said, "Makgar, listen to me. Who knew that Elray was going into the city?"

"No one."

"You said he had to pick up a machine part. Was the time fixed?"

"I suppose so." She looked at him, startled. "Earl! Do you think that Elray—? No. He couldn't. He wouldn't."

There was no limit to what a hungry man would do, and the hunger for money could ruin a world. A date and time arranged, a route chosen, and who would think to blame him? And he had made no attempt to fight the invaders. He had died close to a rifle which could have saved them all. Had the big man paid him off with unexpected coin? A dead man could not talk.

"Earl." Her voice was fading. "Earl."

"Tell me about the boy," he said urgently. "Where should I take him? Who are his people?"

". . . love you," she whispered. "You and me and the boy . . . happiness . . . why did . . . Jondelle!"

"Makgar!"

But she hadn't heard. She had died in the afternoon sunlight with a thin breeze whispering a dirge and the scent of grass like delicate flowers. He had buried her beneath a flowering tree, leaving the useless raft as a marker.

A bad memory best forgotten.

He took a deep breath as he left the Kladour. The professor had been of no help, he had no idea where Elray had arranged to get his part, and the peace officers of the city were uninterested in anything which happened outside of their jurisdiction. There was nothing he could do but wait for the jeweler's messenger at the House of the Gong.

It was in the Narn, a sprawling, brawling place such as he had seen on a hundred worlds. An area filled with places of synthetic joy where men and women drank and gambled and tasted unwise delights. The voices of the touts were a droning susurration.

"See, be seen, watch, and be watched. The erotic fantasies of a thousand worlds assembled for your participation and watchful enjoyment. No limit, one fee, stay as long as you can stand the pace!"

"Honest tables and straight dealing. Free food and wine. Ten chips to leave with no matter what."

"Let the mystic crystals of Muhtua read the things which are to come. Good fortune, good health, and safe passage."

"Real knives! Real blood! Young buckos willing to take on all contenders! A hundred stergals if you stay unmarked for three minutes!" The tout caught Dumarest by the arm. "You, sir. I can tell you're no stranger with a blade. Easy money for a single bout."

With a fixed blade, lights adjusted to dazzle, a spray of numbing gas, perhaps, to slow him down. Dumarest shook off the arm.

"No?" The tout shrugged, sneering. "Afraid of a scratch or two?" He appealed to a group of onlookers. "You there, sir, you with that charming girl at your side. I'll bet ten stergals you have more courage. Ten coins in your hand if you enter the ring and a hundred more if you stay unmarked for three minutes."

He was young, little more than a boy, someone from the

edging farms, perhaps, after a little adult fun. The girl at his side gave him no opportunity to refuse the baited offer.

"Go on, Garfrul. Ten stergals! We could go to the Disaphar and try one of those analogues."

"The little lady has the right idea," shouted the tout. He tweaked the baited hook. "Ten in the hand before you start. A hundred, maybe, when you finish. Think of what you could buy . . . the best food in the Narn, the best wine. A place at the highest table. Who knows, with luck you could turn it into a fortune. It's been done before."

The boy hesitated. "I don't know," he said. "I'm not much use with a knife."

"You're fast," urged his companion. Her eyes were too bright, too eager, a she-cat lusting for excitement. "You can dodge around for a little while. Three minutes isn't long and think of what we could do with the money. A new suit, a new dress, a chance to better yourself. Oh, Garfrul! I'd be so proud of you! I'd tell all the girls— no I won't. If I did they'd be after you and I'm jealous."

Dumarest watched, knowing what was to come. Ten stergals for a slash which would sever tendons and leave the boy maimed for life. A double handful of coins for wounds which would leave permanent scars. An evening of innocent pleasure ruined before it had begun.

Abruptly he said, "Don't be a fool, boy. Don't be led to the slaughter."

The tout turned, snarling. "Why don't you mind your own business? He's old enough to make up his own mind. What's it to you what he does?"

Nothing, but he had blond hair and blue eyes and looked as Jondelle might look if he were lucky enough to stay alive.

To the boy he said, "You want to see what they were leading you into? Then follow me." To the tout he snapped, "I'll take your offer. A hundred stergals for three minutes, you say?"

"If you stay unmarked, yes."

"How much if I win?"

The tout blinked, his eyes wary, but the crowd was pressing close and he could visualize a full house. "Double."

"First blood, no breaks, an empty ring?"

"Sure."

"Then let's get inside."

Dumarest thrust his way into the booth, nose crinkling to familiar scents, blood and sweat and oil, the intangible odor of anticipation and the animal-stink of blood-lust. Behind him came the boy, the girl hugging his arm, her eyes unnaturally bright. After them came the crowd from the street, scenting violence to come, willing to pay the extra the tout demanded for the privilege of watching men cut and slash at each other with naked steel.

They filed into the booth, whispering as Dumarest examined the ring. It was a sanded area, twelve feet square, raised four feet above the floor. Overhead lights threw an eye-bright brilliance. He looked at them, squinting, seeing the other, unlit lights, aimed at each corner of the combat area. The lights which could be flashed to dazzle and bemuse a combatant who proved too dangerous.

"All set?" The tout came forward, smiling, knives in his hands, his champion at his side. He was tall, lithe, dressed only in pants and boots, his naked torso gleaming with oil and laced with the cicatrices of old scars. His hair was close-cropped to a rounded skull and his face, broad, flat-nosed, held the impassivity of an executioner.

"I'm ready," said Dumarest.

"Good. You'll have to strip, but I guess you know that." He watched as Dumarest removed his tunic and handed it to Garfrul. "You've been in a ring before?"

"I've watched a few times and we used to fight a little at a place I worked at once. Practice blades only, of course."

There was no need to lie when a part of the truth would serve as well.

"I thought so," said the tout. "I can tell when a man knows what he's doing. Get in the ring and I'll hand you the blade."

The naked edge was ten inches long, dull, heavy, and ill-balanced. Dumarest poised it, then held out his hand. "I'll take the other one."

"Something wrong?"

"You tell me. No?" Dumarest shrugged and threw aside the knife. "Then I'll use my own." He lifted it from his boot and turned it so the light flashed from the blade. "It's shorter by an inch," he said calmly. "I'm giving your boy an advantage. Now blow the whistle and let's get this over with."

The tout hesitated. "That all right with you, Krom?"

His champion shrugged, confident in his own prowess. "Sure."

Still the man hesitated, looking at Dumarest, his knife, his scars, uneasy at the fear that he had been led into a trap. Then a man yelled from the back of the crowd.

"Come on, there! Where's the action?"

Others took it up, a roar of sound, feral, demanding. Feet began pounding the floor, a rolling drumbeat of angry impatience. The tout sucked in his breath and stepped from the ring. His whistle killed the noise as if it had been cut by a knife.

Krom moved.

He was clever, skilled, moving more for the crowd than anything else, his knife held a little before him, waist-high, the point upward, the blade twisted a little so as to provide a thread of brilliance along the edge. He took a step forward, back, moved sideways, dancing on the balls of his feet, the point lifting, falling, rising again to eye-level. His stance was open, inviting, left hand held far from his body.

From the crowd a woman screamed, her voice brittle with hysteria. "Cut him, mister! Cut him good!"

Dumarest ignored her as he ignored everything but the man before him. Krom was good, a veteran of a thousand combats, his body trained to move by unthinking reflex action, the master of a dozen tricks. A professional who intended to win; but even if he had been a raw amateur, Dumarest would have been just as wary. Too many things could happen during a fight. Little things, a foot slipping, light reflecting from a blade to give temporary blindness, anything. And the luck which had stayed with him so long could even now be running out.

Krom attacked, blade lifted, the edge toward Dumarest's face, moving slower than it should. He caught it on his own knife, the steel clashing, clashing again as he returned the slash, the thin, harsh ringing echoing over the crowd.

Grandstand play to give the effect of savage violence. Korm was acting from habit, aiming at the knife, not at the man, stretching the bout so as to make it look good and to encourage others to test their skill. Dumarest could have cut him then, but he had his own motivations. A fight soon ended looked too easy. He wanted the boy to be sure of what was happening.

He backed, confident that there would be no real attack as yet, but alert just the same. He weaved, seeing the back of the blade turned toward him, allowing it to come closer than it might. He cut, clumsily, deliberately missing, Krom springing out of range with smooth efficiency, blades clashing as he blocked a second attack. Dumarest stooped, knocked up the knife arm, and sent the point of his weapon whining an inch from the glistening chest.

The crowd roared, screaming at the expected sight of blood, quieting as they saw the unmarked torso. A bell rang sharply.

"Minute one!"

They parted, standing at either side of the ring, crouched a little, light on the balls of their feet. Krom's left arm lifted, swept down in a sharp gesture. A signal, perhaps? Dumarest thought of the aimed lights, the other devices used in such a place to insure victory for the champion. Krom must know that his chest could have been cut in the last encounter, and a man of his experience would take no chances.

He came forward, knife held up and out, the blade flickering as it weaved a pattern. An amateur would have tried to follow it, to anticipate where it would be and when it would thrust or cut. Dumarest knew better. He backed, keeping clear, his own knife ready and waiting. He felt the ropes behind him, sprang to one side as Krom lunged forward, sprang again as the man turned and swept up the knife. He caught it on his own, lifted, and stared into the broad face.

Krom jerked up his knee.

Dumarest twisted, felt it slam against his thigh, and pushed hard against the trapped knife. Krom staggered back, off balance and temporarily helpless. Dumarest sprang after him, saw the uplifted blade, the tiny hole below the edge in the guard. He turned in midair, landing like a cat, leaping to the side of the ring as the invisible spray lashed toward him. Krom followed it, holding his breath, cutting upward so as to hit the wrist and slash the tendons. The knives jarred, held, broke free as Dumarest sprang to the center of the ring.

Above the sighing inhalation of the crowd he heard the harsh clang of the bell.

"Minute two!"

A lie, of course; the tout would be stretching the time. But lie or not, one thing was certain: the playacting was over. And more than playacting. Krom had used his spray, the puff of gas which would stun and slow, and while Dumarest remained in the center of the ring the lights could not be used. Now it was just one against the other with naked steel and skill, luck and speed deciding the winner.

Krom attacked, feinting, changing the direction of his cut, backing as the blades clashed to attack again. Dumarest moved in a tight circle, turned a little so as to present his knife-side to his opponent, mentally counting seconds. Twenty . . . Krom would be getting desperate. Thirty . . . now, if at all, he would put out his major effort. A trick he had learned, perhaps, a baffling move which had proven worthwhile.

From the crowd a woman shrieked.

It was a scream of utter agony, rising, demanding immediate attention. It shocked the crowd. It would have shocked any amateur fighter, causing him to turn, to expose himself for the necessary second to be cut.

Dumarest didn't turn. He knew the distraction to be what it was. Before him Krom's knife flashed, vanished, flashed again in his other hand. It came forward like a finger of light as his right hand lifted in an empty feint. Dumarest moved to his right, his left forearm slamming against Krom's left wrist, his own knife moving out to gently cut a shallow gash on the naked shoulder.

"Blood!" a man yelled at the sight. "He's cut him! He's won!"

The bout was over. Dumarest should have relaxed, lowered his knife, turned, perhaps, to the crowd in smiling victory. Turned—and taken Krom's knife in his kidneys.

He had won—but a dead man could collect no winnings and who would care about a stranger?

He saw the man turn, the knife back in his right hand, the point lifting to stab at his heart. Dumarest caught the wrist, fingers locking like iron around the flesh and sinew, halting the blade an inch from his skin. His own knife rose, the edge hard against the corded throat.

"Drop it!" he said and then, as Krom hesitated, "Don't be a fool, man! You've lost, but you can live to fight again!"

"Fast," muttered Krom. "Too damn fast. You could

have taken me in the first ten seconds. Althen was a fool to have picked you." The knife fell from his hand. "You're a pro. Anyone else would have killed me. Now what?"

"Nothing," said Dumarest. "I'm going to collect."

Jumping from the ring, he snatched his tunic from the boy's hands and headed to the box office. The tout was busy. He cringed as Dumarest caught his arm.

"Now wait a minute. There's no need to get rough. I was just checking the take."

"You owe me two hundred stergals. I want it."

"Sure, but—" Althen dabbed at his sweating face. "Look—you're a reasonable man. You know how we operate. Ten stergals, yes, but how can I pay more? I've expenses, the concession to pay for, other things. Profits are low and getting lower all the time. Tell you what, I'll settle for fifty."

Dumarest tightened his hand.

"You cheated me. You conned me into a trap. You had Krom beaten from the whistle." He looked at Dumarest's hard eyes, the cruel mouth. "I can pay," Althen admitted. "Just. But if you take it, you'll ruin me."

"Damn you," said Dumarest harshly. "What is that to me?"

CHAPTER

SEVEN

There were baths of steam and scented water, a masseuse with hands like petals with fingers of steel as she probed and eased the tension from skin and muscle. Her voice was a tempting whisper.

"You wish delights, master? A girl to beguile you, chemicals to maintain your interest, visual effects to increase your enjoyment. No? An analogue, perhaps? To experience what it is to wear another form, to mate in the shape of a beast, to hunt and kill, to feed—we have a wide variety. Still no? Then to sit and experience death in a dozen different ways. Sensitapes recorded with full stimuli from those who have burned, have fallen, have been slowly crushed. Or other things— No? As you please, master. You will sleep a little, then? An hour of blissful peace induced by the microcurrents at hand. No? Then rest, master, and let your thoughts wander. The bell will summon me in case of need."

The bell which commanded every joy invented by man—at a price.

Dumarest ignored it, lying supine, looking at the painted ceiling and the images it contained. Vague scenes summoned from the abstract design and fashioned by the power of his mind. Armored figures limned by flame, savage faces, another with a rim of blood around the mouth. Hair of jet, of gold, of brilliant flame. Women he had met and loved and lost. Worlds he had seen, the stars, a monstrous shape robed in scarlet engulfing them in a web. A boy with golden hair and vivid blue eyes.

Damn Garfrul. He had looked too much like Jondelle and he had been a fool. It had been stupid to interfere, more than stupid to fight. And he had shown the boy nothing except what seemed to be an easy way to make money. He would practice, think himself strong, and pay for it with vicious cuts.

His girl would see to that.

Dumarest remembered her face, the planes and contours framed by a wealth of midnight hair, the eyes which had betrayed her selfish nature. And yet was she so wrong to reach for what she desired? Lallia had been a little like that, strong and ruthless in her fashion, knowing what she wanted and honest enough to admit it. Lallia who had died on a world in the Web, killed by an agent of the Cyclan.

He thought again of the scarlet shape engulfing worlds. The symbol of the organization which sought complete domination of the galaxy. Its agents spreading to influence every sphere of importance. The cybers who were living robots devoid of all emotion, who could only know the pleasure of mental achievement. Men who had been taken as boys, to be trained, operated on, the thalamus divorced from the cortex, so they could never experience hate or love or fear. Creatures in human form who could take a handful of data and extrapolate from it in lines of logical sequence and so predict the outcome of any course of action.

The Cyclan which hunted him and would always hunt him as long as he held the secret of the affinity twin given to him by Kalin. Kalin of the flame-red hair. Red robes, red gems, red the color of blood which had stained his path for as long as he could remember.

But there were no cybers on Ourelle. The culture was too splintered, too divided, without strong government or rulers of influence. Ourelle, a backward world, almost ignored, an easy place in which to get lost.

Was that why Makgar had chosen it?

Dumarest turned again, restless, unable to wholly relax. The ceiling held too many images, inspired too many trains of thought . . . Jondelle and what might be happening to him . . . what could happen unless he was found. Why was he so concerned with the boy?

A promise given to dying woman. His word. It was enough.

To the air he said, "What is the time?"

"Three hours before midnight," a soft voice responded. "The night is dry but there is cloud."

Time to be moving. Outside the baths he paused and looked at the blaze of light which hung like a nimbus over the Narn. More light shone from where the field lay beyond the city, floodlights which showed every inch

f ground with the perimeter fence. As he watched
here was a crack of displaced air from high above and a
hip, wreathed in the blue halo of its Erhaft drive,
ettled to the ground below.

A ship, small, probably engrossed in local trade, but
vessel he could take, the cash in his pocket buying him
High passage to where there would be other ships
haking longer journeys. But no ship he knew could take
im where he wanted to go.

A woman said, "You look lonely, friend. That ship
emind you of home? Why don't you come to my place
nd tell me all about it."

"Thank you, no."

"Not in the mood?" She shrugged. "Well, that's the
ay it goes."

She moved on and he walked to the House of the
jong.

It was large, bright, hung with a thousand lanterns
n every shade and combination of color. Suspended
ongs throbbed softly to the impact of an artificial wind
nd a larger gong, pierced, formed the entrance which
vas reached by a flight of low, broad steps. At their foot
cowled figure held a bowl of chipped plastic. Before
im a plump man with his gemmed woman roared with
udden mirth.

"Charity? I don't believe in it. A man should stand
n his own two feet and not depend on alms. Give me
ne good reason why I should put anything into your
owl."

The monk was of the Universal Church, drab in his
homespun robe, feet bare in crude sandals. Within the
cowl his face was lined, pinched by age and deprivation,
ut his eyes were young and bright with infinite compassion.

Quietly he said, "You are about to tempt good fortune,
brother. May luck attend you. But think of those who
have no luck and who lack for bread. It is summer now
out winter will be with us soon. A bad time, brother, for
hose who have no money or friends."

"Not good enough." The plump man shook his head.
"I'm still not convinced."

"You are a gambler, brother, and as such believe in
ymbols and omens. Who knows what brings good for-
une? Your first stake thrown to the ground? Your first

win tossed to the servants? A wise man would surely
make a small sacrifice before he begins to play."

The woman said, "He could be right, Enex. Help
threw a beggar a coin once and won a thousand stergals.

A good psychologist, thought Dumarest as the plump
man reached into his pocket. But the monks are past
masters of the art. Throwing a coin into the bowl, he
mounted the stairs.

Inside it was warm with gusts of scented air driving
coils of colored smoke past lanterns hanging from the
decorated ceilings. The place was as he expected, tables
for cards, dice, spinning wheels. The games too were
familiar: high-low-man-in-between, poker, spectrum, sevens, starburn, brenzo. A transparent, tube-like container
held a mass of writhing spores, the voice of the house-
man a steady drone.

"The battle commences. Bet now on your choice of
red, blue, or green. The photometer will tell which color
is ascendent at the expiration of sixty seconds. Bet now.
No more bets. Play commences."

He pressed a lever. Nutrients flooded into the container, the spores eating, breeding, fighting, and dying.

"Yellow wins!" The container spun, emptied, grew
bright with fresh spores. "The battle commences. Make
your bets. The photometer . . ."

Dumarest passed on. A girl, dressed from throat to
ankle in a clinging gown of embroidered silk, offered him
a tray of food and drink. Hollow pastries and strong
wine. Fuddled men made careless gamblers.

He waved her aside and headed for the restaurant.
Akon Batik would be in no hurry to send his messenger.
It would be good business to keep him waiting, gambling, perhaps, losing some of the money he had received
for the chorismite. There would be time and to spare
for a meal and Dumarest had early learned to eat while
food was available. A traveler never could be sure when
he would be able to eat again.

He ordered meat, light vegetables, cheese, and a weak
wine. The meat was good and he ate it slowly. The
cheese held a strange pungency and was speckled with seeds
which dissolved to a tart liquid. The wine was dry, scented
with roses, pink with streaks of red. He was emptying
the bottle when a man slipped into the chair opposite.

"Dumarest? Earl Dumarest?"

Dumarest nodded.

"Akin Tambolt. You're expecting me."

"I am?"

"Sure. The jeweler sent me."

"Name him."

Tambolt laughed with a flash of strong, white teeth. "You're cautious; well, I can't blame you. In Sargone most things can happen and usually do. All right, let's use names. Akon Batik, good enough?"

He was young with a hard maturity about the eyes and mouth. A broad, thickset figure which would later run to fat unless he were careful. He was dressed in thick, serviceable clothing, pants and high boots, a shirt of ebon scratched to reveal flashes of the wire mesh beneath. A traveler's garb, or that worn by a man used to rough living. His hands were broad, strong, the nails blunt. One cheek bore a thin scar. His hair was thick, low over ears and neck, brown flecked with auburn. He wore a heavy signet ring on the little finger of each hand. Wide metal bands set with sharp stones. Serviceable weapons for a man who knew how to use them.

A bravo, thought Dumarest. An opportunist. A man who lived on the fringe and would do anything for gain.

Tambolt said, "There was talk of money. Twenty tergals."

"Ten."

"Ten it is, but you can't blame me for trying. Give."

"For what? Because you ask?"

"Do you want to learn what I know or not?"

"I'll find out," said Dumarest. "One way or another, I'll find out. You want to bet on it?"

For a moment their eyes locked, then Tambolt shrugged. "One day, perhaps," he said flatly. "But not now. How 'bout some wine?"

Dumarest ordered a bottle and watched as the other poured himself a glass. "To your health, Earl. Have you eaten?"

"Yes."

"A pity, I'm starving." He called to the waitress and ordered. "You've no objection?"

"None," said Dumarest.

"That's generous of you, Earl. I like a generous man."

"I'm not generous," said Dumarest. "Just impatient. What have you to tell me?"

"Nothing. That is nothing which seems to be of use. The jeweler passed the word and asked in the right places. No one seems to have hired bravos to steal the boy. The lads you took care of in the city must have come from outside. That or no one admits to ever having seen them before. The others, those that hit you at the farm, no the Melevganians, the same."

The food came and he ate with a barely masked hunger.

"Of course the sources could be lying, but I don't think so. Akon is in well with everyone who matters and Sargone isn't all that large. People listen, they learn, and they talk if they can gain by it. Whoever wanted the boy must have played it close. They could have used their own men, in which case you're up a dead end."

"Perhaps not," said Dumarest. "The husband, Elray, could have told someone where and when he would be. The attack in the city doesn't make sense otherwise. No one would have known when to hit."

"The husband?" Tambolt swallowed the last of his meal. "You think he agreed to have his boy stolen?"

"Jondelle wasn't his child. He was dependent on his wife and maybe he wanted to make a break. If the opportunity was there, he could have taken it."

"Money for the child, some pretended grief, and then a quiet disappearance." Tambolt nodded. "It could have been done that way, but who would be willing to pay in order to get the boy? Usually it's the other way around. Steal the child and demand ransom."

"Yes."

"Which makes you think and gives rise to some interesting speculation. The boy must have a high value for someone. Perhaps whoever stole him knows the market and what the goods will bring. But you've thought of that, of course."

"Yes," said Dumarest again.

"Which maybe accounts for your interest? I'd wondered. You aren't related to the boy, so what's it to you if he gets stolen? But if you knew where the market was—"

"If I did I wouldn't be wasting time here," said Dumarest curtly.

"Maybe. Or maybe you know where it is and want to have the goods to hand." Tambolt sucked at his teeth. "Say, that meat was good. Mind if I have some more?"

"Eat as much as you like—you're paying for it."

"What?"

"From the money you hope to get from me. The ten tergals promised. It's down to seven now."

"Damn you!" Tambolt's hand clenched into a fist, light splintering on the sharp point of the gem in his ring. "You can't do that to me!"

"No?" Dumarest smiled without amusement. "Did you think I was so easy to con? Grow up, man. So far you haven't told me anything of value. You're a messenger, all right, so maybe it isn't your fault. But don't expect me to be grateful." Deliberately he reached for the bottle of wine and helped himself. "Your health. From the way you ate that meat things haven't been too good lately."

"You can say that again." Tambolt took a deep breath and unclenched his hand. "So I made a mistake," he admitted. "I tried to get more than was due and fell flat on my face. Well, it's a lesson."

He refilled his glass and sat back nursing the wine, looking older than he had, more haggard. A man who had dressed to a part, who had tried to live up to it and who now tasted the bitter fruit of failure.

"Akon gave me the job," he said. "I didn't know who or what you were—well, that doesn't matter now. How keen are you to find the boy?"

"Produce him and I'll give you the cost of a High passage."

"Traveler's talk. The way you assess values. Riding Low, High, Middle when you can get a berth on a vessel. You traveled much?"

"Yes."

"I've done a little. Not much, a couple of worlds, just enough to know that luck rides against me. I saw a man who had taken one chance too many on my last trip. When they opened the casket he was dead. Young too, younger than me. Ourelle seemed to hold promise, so I stayed. Now I haven't the price of a decent meal." He sipped at his wine. "Would you think that I've got a degree in geology?"

Dumarest was curt. "Does it matter?"

"What do you think? No, not really. Only I know rocks and formations and I've done a little prospecting. I've studied Ourelle, too, had a job in the Kladour for a while. They fired me because—well, never mind. Just say that we didn't see eye to eye on expenses. Field trips can come

high. And I found a few things I didn't turn in." Tambo
looked at his rings. "Nice stones, aren't they? Fakes, c
course, but they'd pass a casual inspection. Only th
Kladour doesn't make casual inspections. I tried to buil
up the stake at the tables and lost the lot. One day I'
learn. When I'm dead maybe. When it's too late."

He emptied his glass and refilled it, gulping half c
it in a single swallow as if making a defiant gesture t
some private devil. Greed, perhaps, or inadequacy, o
an intellectual blindness which made him underestimat
all he met. Or, thought Dumarest grimly, he could b
lying, presenting a facade he hoped would appeal.

Bluntly he said, "The boy?"

"You want to find him. Maybe I can help you."

"How?"

"You know, Earl. You must have thought of it.
guess you think of most things. Melevganians attacked th
farm, but they weren't alone. The strangers took the boy
Where? We don't know. Who were they? We don't know
that either. But maybe the Melevganians do. So reach
them and make them talk. Right?"

He poured more wine as Dumarest made no answer.

"I'm beginning to understand why the jeweler picked
me to carry his message. He's old and shrewd and car
see the obvious. You want to go to Melevgan, there are
gems there, things of value, and he knows we'd take him
what we found. Fat profits and no risk. No wonder
he's rich."

Dumarest said, flatly, "I'm after the boy, not a handfu
of stones."

"You could get both—or get neither. You think i
easy? Going to Melevgan isn't like taking a stroll in
the park. I've been there and I know. One wrong move
and you'll wind up dead. You need me, Earl. Partners?"

Dumarest leaned back, sipping at his wine. From beyond the dining area came the susurration of gamblers
at their play, the rattle of dice, the inhalations, cries of joy,
and expressions of disgust. Devotees of the goddess of
chance. Trying their luck as all men had to try it in
order to stay alive. Yet not always were the odds so
great. Most could pick their gambles, others could not.
Jondelle for one.

He said, "What would we need?"

"A raft. Trade goods. Weapons and men. It won't come cheap."

"A thousand?"

"Not enough." Tambolt was emphatic. "A raft comes high—no one will rent one out so you'll have to buy. Trade goods will take half of it, weapons more, and then you'll have to find some men. They'll want high pay."

Dumarest thought of the farm and what he had left there. There and on the way to the city. He said, "We don't need a raft, only an engine. We can hire one with a driver to take us out to the farm. What do they need in the way of trade goods?"

"The Melevganians? Manufactured items; missiles for their lances, some electronic circuitry, drills, machine tools, stuff like that. The money will cover it, the engine too, but what about the men?"

Dumarest finished his wine. "I'll get the men."

CHAPTER

EIGHT

It was going to rain. Brother Elas could tell from the ache in his bones, the sure sign of inclement weather and soon would come the winter, the snows from the north and the bitter, freezing winds. On Ourelle seasons were short and all too soon the sultry days of summer would be over, the sun hidden by cloud, the ground hard and misery rampant. A bad time for monks as well as penitents. A bleak time for those who had nowhere to turn for aid but the church.

The thought of it made him shiver; imagination, of course, for the night was warm and the rain would do no more than bring wetness. But funds, as always, were low and he knew too well what was to come. Well, it was a thing that could not be helped and would have to be accepted along with the rest. With his duties, for one, and they were something which could not be shirked.

He walked slowly from the hut to where the church stood on a patch of waste ground. Small as such churches always were, a prefabricated structure built up with flimsy sheeting, the body containing his seat, the benediction light, the place for the suppliant. Brother Karl came to meet him, his young face showing signs of fatigue. Bowing, he said, "We are busy tonight, Brother."

"That is bad?"

"No, but—"

"You are tired."

"True, but even so—"

"You are tired," repeated the elder monk firmly. "A dull brain sees things not always as they are. You must eat and rest a little, and, Brother, remember what you are and why you are here."

A rebuke but a mild one, yet necessary just the same. The sin of impatience was close to that of pride and no monk of the Universal Church must ever forget for a moment that he was a servant and not a master. That his duty was to help and never to demand. To learn that frustration was a part of life and his task seemingly endless.

Not an easy thing to accept, less so when the body was young and the soul restless. And yet Brother Karl would learn as they all had learned that the universe could not be altered in a day. That it was enough to take one penitent and give ease and comfort and to instill the creed which was the reason for their being. The one concept which alone could bring true happiness.

"There, but for the grace of God, go I."

Once all men accepted it, lived by it, the millennium would be at hand.

Brother Karl bowed, humiliated. "My apologies, Brother. I have still to learn."

"You have learned, but at times you forget to remember. Now go and eat a little and rest for a while. A fatigued body makes a bad servant and you have worked hard."

Too hard, he thought, as the young man moved away. Trying to do everything at once and yielding to irritation at the apparent slowness of progress. It was nothing new. All monks felt the same when they left the great seminary on the planet Hope, eager to take what they had learned and convert it into living fact. But he would learn as they all had learned that patience was the greatest weapon they possessed. Patience and dedication and, above all an infinite compassion.

He took his place in the church, bones creaking as he dropped into the still-warm seat. How long had it been since he had listened to his first suppliant? Forty years . . . it must be at least that, probably more. Almost a half century since he had gone to his first station to work with other, older monks, absorbing what they could teach, treading the path they had shown. He could have been the resident head now of an established church somewhere on a hospitable world, but always he had chosen to move on, to work at the beginnings, to go where he considered he was needed most.

Hard worlds. A hard life, but he would have chosen no other.

He blinked, conscious that his mind was wandering, and straightened, touching the bell to summon the first of the waiting suppliants. The man was thin, his skin febrile, his eyes unnaturally bright. He knelt before the benediction light, the waves of color laving his face with kaleidoscopic brilliance. His voice was a hurried murmur.

". . . and I took what wasn't mine. I stole a cloak and a pair of boots and sold them and kept the money. I was going to buy food but there was this place and I thought I could make it more so I gambled it and lost it and when I got back the baby had died. The money would have saved it, maybe. But I tried, Brother. I know I did wrong but I tried and now . . ."

Tormented by guilt he had turned to the only surcease he knew.

"Look into the light," said Brother Elas. "Let the light of forgiveness cleanse away your sin and bring ease to your heart. Look into the light."

The wash of color which induced a rapid hypnotic trance. The men would suffer subjective penance and rise to take the bread of forgiveness.

Others came, a stream of them with their petty crimes, most inventing their sins in order to receive the wafer of concentrates which helped them stay alive. Brother Elas did not mind; it was a small price to pay for the prohibition against killing instilled by the light. Smaller to embrace them in the body of Humanity, the great Brotherhood of Man where each should be the other's keeper and no man need live alone.

It was a long session, but finally it ended, no one answering the summons of the bell. Stiffly the old monk rose and left the church. It had begun to rain, a thin drizzle which made the ground slippery beneath his sandals, and increased the ache in his bones. Brother Karl, his face smoother now, his eyes less harassed, met him as he neared his hut.

"You have a visitor, Brother. I asked him to wait."

"Has he been here long?"

"Less than an hour. I would have called you, but he insisted that I should not. Shall I attend you?"

"No. Close the church; there will be no more penitents tonight. But if you could prepare me a little food . . . ?"

Dumarest rose as the monk entered the hut. He had been studying a fabrication of seeds and scraps of shining mineral, the whole worked into the likeness of a young man, robed, the cowl thrown back over his shoulders. Introducing himself, he said, "You, Brother?"

"Yes." Elas touched it, his thin hand gentle on the

ornate workmanship. "A memento from Kalgarsh. You
know the world?"

"No."

"A hard place of poor soil and scanty crops. I was
there very many years ago now. The women are deft and
I tried to introduce a new art-form, souvenirs which they
could sell to the tourists who came to watch the storms.
The ground is arid, the winds strong and, at certain times
of the year, vast clouds of colored dust hang like images
in the sky. They gave me this when I left."

"A thoughtful tribute," said Dumarest politely.

"A small thing, but I value it. Vain, perhaps, but it
is not always wise to forget the past and, at my age,
memories hold undue tenderness. And now, brother, you
have business with me?"

"I need your help."

"Mine, brother?"

"Yours and that of the Church." Dumarest told him
of the boy and what had happened. "The mystery is why
he should have been stolen at all. He belonged, as far as
I know, to no rich House. Certainly his mother had little
wealth. As a slave he would be of little worth and no
slaver would have gone to so much trouble. He has been
taken somewhere. I want to know where. If I knew why
he was taken in the first place, it could help me to find
him."

"I see." The old monk sat, brooding. "And your own
interest?"

"A promise to his dying mother." Dumarest guessed
what the other was thinking. "I can't keep the boy with
me. If he has relatives, he must go to where he belongs.
But I don't intend that those who stole him should keep
him. They have too much to answer for. Perhaps, with
luck, I shall make them pay for what they have done."

"With death," said Elas bitterly. "With maiming and
violence and physical hurt. You are a hard man, Dumarest.
Perhaps too hard. But how can I help you?"

"You and the Universal Church," corrected Dumarest.
"You have monks on almost every world and I know the
influence you have on those in high places. Friends who
would be willing to help, if only to answer a question
or two. And there could be others looking for the boy.
You could ask, find out if such a boy is missing from
his family, find his relatives, perhaps. Anything."

"And how could this be done?"

"You know, Brother. We both know."

By means of the hyper-radio incorporated into every benediction light, a network of communication which spread across the galaxy. To Hope itself where records were kept and the answer could, perhaps, be found.

"A boy," said Dumarest. "Young, lost, in peril of his life, perhaps. Someone who needs your help and the help you can give. I know that you cannot refuse."

Brother Elas sighed. The man was right, of course; he could not refuse, but there was so little to go on. A boy, young, blond, blue-eyed—the description would fit so many.

"Is there nothing else you can tell me? Was he born here on Ourelle?"

"I don't think so. His mother could have brought him from Veido—I don't know the planet."

"No solidiograph or list of physical peculiarities?" The monk spread his hands. "You can appreciate the difficulties. The more information I have, the better I will be able to help."

"I understand," said Dumarest. "And I think I can get you what you need. But I did not come here simply to ask. I have an offer as well. Make no mistake about what I am next going to say. I know that you cannot be bribed and need no payment for what I ask you to do. In fact, I'm going to ask even more."

"Yes?"

"The boy's mother owned a farm. She is dead now, her husband too. The title goes to the boy, but he is young and may never be found. I ask you to hold it in trust for him until it can be claimed. There is damage, but the house is intact and the crops ready for harvesting. There is water and plentiful timber. No one will argue if you choose to take it over and work it."

Elas said quietly, "You swear that what you have told me is the truth?"

"I am known on Hope. The High Monk Jerome will vouch for me."

"He is dead. Didn't you know?"

"The records, then."

The records which never died; the prospect was enticing. Elas sat back, thinking about it. A farm to provide food, warmth, and comfort against the bleakness to come. Shelter against the iron grip of winter. Brother Karl could handle it and find a vent for his energies in doing so. A place in which men could work and gain strength and recover their self-respect. A haven for the families who had no hope.

Dumarest rose. "You will need to think about it. I hope to leave within a few hours. A hired raft will take me to the farm. If you will send a monk, he can see the place and make his report. Also, I may be able to give more details about the boy. The raft, of course, will carry the monk back to you."

"Brother Karl will accompany you. And now?"

"Now," said Dumarest flatly, "I have to find some men."

They were where he expected them to be, crouched under scraps of plastic sheeting and hammered fragments of metal, discarded planks and strips of various materials. Poor protection against the rain, but all they had. The stranded, the travelers who lacked the price of a Low passage, those who had for some reason or other found themselves at the bottom of the heap. The desperate.

A man sat under an awning stirring a pot which stood over a smoldering fire. He looked up as Dumarest passed, his eyes suspicious, wary. Behind him a woman coughed and drew a moldy blanket tighter around her shoulders. Two others threw dice with blank interest, killing time with nothing to stake. A group huddled close for mutual comfort. A man pursed his lips as he mended a ragged tear in a boot. Another honed the blade of a knife.

Lowtowns were all the same.

Dumarest walked through it, catching the stench, the scent of dirt and bad health, of poor food and corrosive despair. And everywhere was the unmistakable stink of poverty.

He halted, lifting his voice.

"I want some men. An engineer able to repair a raft. Others with strong backs and shoulders. Who's interested?"

The man honing the knife rose and slipped the blade into a sheath at his waist.

"For what?"

"A journey. It's hard and rough and so I want men to match. You'll get food, clothing, and maybe the price of a passage when the job is done."

"High or Low?"

"Maybe High."

The man frowned. "Maybe?"

"That's what I said." Dumarest met his eyes, turned to look at the others who had clustered around. The man with the torn boot pressed close.

"I'm an engineer. You want a raft fixed, I can do it."

"You sure about that?"

"I'm sure." The man's eyes shifted a little. "You just give me the chance and I'll show you what I can do. You don't have to believe me, ask the monks, they'll tell you what I can do."

"You've been under the light?"

"Why, sure, how else could—"

"Forget it," snapped Dumarest. "Anyone else?"

A squat man thrust himself forward. He wore drab clothing, patched boots, and a mended shirt, but his cheeks were full and his shoulders square. He said, "I'm called Jasken. You want a good engineer, I'm your man. I can build a raft from scrap and if you want mining gear fixed, I can do that too. And I'm religious."

A man called, "What difference does it make?"

"He wents men who can fight and kill if they have to." Jasken didn't take his eyes off Dumarest. "All right, I'm willing to do anything to get a stake. What's your proposition?"

"I told you. Food, clothing, money if we find it, nothing if we don't."

"A journey. To where?" He whistled as Dumarest told him. "Hell, I've heard of that place. Mister, you don't know what you're asking!"

"Did I say it would be easy?" Dumarest shrugged. "I'm no monk and I'm not offering charity. I'm giving you a chance to get out of this stink and try your luck on some other world. You're an engineer, you say?"

"A good one."

"You'd better be. If you're lying, you'll regret it."

Jasken drew in his breath. "I don't lie, mister. I don't have to."

"Then why aren't you working? No rafts to be repaired on Ourelle? No mines with equipment to be kept operating? Tell me."

"They've got guilds. You belong to one or you don't work. Outside Sargone, maybe, but how do I get there? I landed three months ago after riding Low. I've worked maybe three weeks. Cut-rate jobs, but I was glad to get

them. Then the guilds moved in and passed the word—
employ me and ask for trouble. No one wants trouble."
Jasken bared his teeth. "I've managed to stay alive, but it
hasn't been easy, and I'd go to hell and back for a High
passage."

"That's what I'm asking."

"Then that's what you'll get. Jasken looked at Dumarest,
his eyes searching. "You're a traveler, I can tell. Haven't
you ever been stranded? Don't you know what it's like?"

"I know," said Dumarest shortly.

"Yes, I guess you do. How many men do you need? I
know them," he added as Dumarest made no answer.
"I know who uses the Church and who doesn't The
strong from the weak, those with the guts to take a chance
and those who just want to sit and wait for a miracle.
You'll let me pick them?"

His friends, those he could trust to back him if it
came to trouble? Desperate men wouldn't be squeamish if
offered a chance to make some easy money. It was a chance
he was reluctant to take and yet Dumarest knew there
was little choice. No matter whom he picked, they would
have a common cause.

He said, "Pick about eight. I'll sort them out. Have
them stand over by the church." As Jasken moved off,
he returned to where the man sat before his pot of stew
and stared down at him. "You. What's your name?"

"Preleret. Why?"

"Get on your feet!"

For a moment the man hesitated, than slowly rose, his
eyes glinting.

"Listen, mister—I may not be much, but I don't get
pushed around. Not by you. Not by anyone."

"Is that your woman?"

The man glanced to where she sat, shivering despite
the warmth of the night.

"I'm looking after her."

"She's dying," said Dumarest bluntly. "In a week all
you'll be able to do for her is to put her in the ground.
I offered you a job, why didn't you take it?"

Deliberately the man spat. "I've been conned before,
mister. Work hard, keep loyal, and collect the pot at the
end of the rainbow. To hell with it. On Frendis I worked
for six weeks gathering the harvest and found I owed
more at the end of it than I'd earned. On Carsburg three

months on a construction gang with the promise of a fat
bonus, overtime, and double pay on holidays. There was
no bonus, no overtime, and no damn holidays. You know
what I got out of it? A new pair of boots. To hell with
promises!"

"And her?" Dumarest jerked his head at the woman.
"To hell with her too?"

"Damn you! Don't you think I know how bad she is?
What are you trying to do?"

Dumarest dug coins from his pocket, let them clink
in his palm. "This will save her," he said quietly. "Money
to buy her the drugs and attention she needs. A place
in the infirmary, food to build her up, put flesh on her
bones. Are you too proud to take it?"

"Mister, where she's concerned I'd eat dirt. No, I've
got no pride."

"I want you to come with me," said Dumarest. "All
I can offer you is a chance—but what have you got now?
Nothing. She'll die and you'll follow." He handed over
the money. "I'm not bribing you; the money's yours
whether you come or not. But think about it. If you want
to come, I'll be back here at noon."

"I—" The man swallowed, staring at the money.
"Mister, I—"

"Noon." said Dumarest. "At the church."

He walked away to where Jasken waited with the men
he had selected. Preleret would be at the rendezvous,
despite what he'd said, he had pride and would be
grateful. The touch of the money would work its magic,
what it could do and what more could bring. Health,
escape and, perhaps, happiness. He would be there and
would provide a little insurance against the rest. The others
to be picked from those Jasken had chosen.

CHAPTER
NINE

The farm looked as he remembered, the house with closed windows looking like blind eyes, the door still closed by the planks he had nailed across the panel. Before it lay the ash from the fires, spread now, evened out by the wind so as to give the appearance of dingy snow. The invaders lay where they had fallen, bizarre armor dusted with gray, blown ash heaped in little drifts to blend them with the ground.

Dumarest studied the area. A mound of dirt showed where the Hegelt had buried their dead, a smaller one beside it where he had buried Elray. All was covered with ash. There were no footprints. The small, dark people had mourned their dead and then departed, driven away by fear of ghosts or later vengeance. They had been leaving when he had nursed the raft toward the city.

Brother Karl said, "An ugly scene, brother. It does not belong in such a gentle place."

"No."

"Shall we land?"

"A moment." Dumarest called to Tambolt where he rode with the others in the repaired raft. "Make a swing about the area. A large one, out to those trees on the ridge. I want to make sure no one is lurking about."

"You expect trouble?" The driver of the hired raft pulled uneasily at the collar of his shirt. "Now look, mister. I was hired to carry you out and then lift the monk back to the city. Nobody said anything about heading into a war."

Dumarest said, "Land close to the house. A few feet before the front door."

"Shall I start to unload?"

"Yes." Dumarest glanced at the bales in the body of the vehicle, the trade goods Tambolt had purchased. "But be careful. Drop one and we could all go sky-high."

"Explosives? But—"

"Just be careful."

The planks yielded with a squeal. Dumarest threw them aside and walked into the familiar area. It was dim, light streaming past him through the open door throwing vague shadows in the passage and foot of the stairs. They vanished as he opened more doors, filling the house with an emerald luminescence.

"A fine house," said the monk. His eyes were bright, eager. Already he was mentally allocating quarters and evaluating what needed to be done. That room for the administration, that for the benediction light, another to dispense medicines. Trees could be cut to provide timber for shacks. Clay could be dug, molded, and fired for drainage pipes and an extension of the water supply. Baths could hug the river, the silos repaired, the sheds, the workshops. Stone and mud to provide extensions to the house. The materials were at hand and they would not be short of labor. "A fine dwelling," he said again. "A haven for those in need during the winter."

"To be held in trust," Dumarest reminded. "For the boy."

"Of course, that is understood." Brother Karl looked at the ugly stains on the floor of the room in which they stood. "The owner died here?"

"The owner's husband. She died on the way to the city. You saw her grave."

"Of course, I should have remembered. Well, where shall we begin?"

The room was a study, the desk filled with scraps of paper, old bills, records, lists of plantings and stores. Dumarest looked at a folded document, the title to the farm, and learned from it nothing he did not already know. He handed it to the monk and stood, frowning.

"The boy was close to her," he said. "Upstairs, perhaps, in her room?"

It held memories he did his best to ignore. Hours spent in bandaging, cooling fevered skin, of replacing covers thrown aside. A wardrobe held an assortment of clothing, serviceable gowns, mostly, thick coats with hoods, strong boots for use in mud. A shimmer of color revealed a low-cut, narrow-waisted dress of diaphanous material. A party dress or one worn by a woman attending a high function. The fabric of the neck and waist was frayed as if adornments had been torn from their foundation.

Gems, perhaps? The jewels which had provided the money to buy the farm?

Dumarest delved into a small chest and found a litter of cosmetics, paint, brushes, vials of perfume.

"The boy's room, perhaps?" suggested the monk.

It was small, snug under the eaves, warm and bright with gay color. Animals of a dozen varieties traced in glowing pigments on the walls, soft covers on the rumpled bed, a shelf which held an assortment of toys, things carved from wood, made of stuffed fabrics, combinations of stones and seeds.

His clothes looked very small.

Dumarest checked everything, his jaw hard, muscles prominent along the line of bone. Jondelle had been asleep, lost, maybe, in childish dreams when the attack had come. He would have woken, frightened, perhaps calling for help. And then the brutal shape of the armored man, grotesque, terrifying, bursting through the door. An arm to clamp him hard against the unyielding chest, a gloved hand rammed over his mouth. And then the sting of the drug which had made him lax, unconscious, easy to handle.

He felt a hand touch his arm. The monk was anxious.

"Is anything wrong? You look—"

"Nothing." Dumarest drew a deep breath into his lungs. "Nothing is wrong."

"Your face—" Brother Karl shook his head. "Your expression. I have seen such before, brother . . . on the face of a man intent on murder." He paused, then added, "There is nothing here. The dispensary, perhaps?"

It was white, clean, a table which could serve as an emergency operating theater, a sterilizing unit to one side, ultraviolet lamps to cleanse the air of harmful bacteria. A cabinet holding drugs, disarranged from Dumarest's earlier searching. Records of treatments given.

He found his own and tore it into tiny fragments as the monk examined the rest.

"Nothing." The monk looked baffled. "And yet she must have treated him, examined him at least. Small children are subject to minor injuries and, as a doctor, she would have been interested in the progress of her child. And why no solidiographs? There isn't a likeness of the boy in the house."

"She was a woman," said Dumarest thoughtfully. "A doctor too, but first a woman."

He went back upstairs and found the chest with its
litter of cosmetics. He tilted it, strewing its contents
on the floor, fingers stiff as he probed the bottom. With
sudden impatience he lifted his clenched hand and slammed
it down hard against the base. Wood cracked, splintered
as he tore it free. The monk edged close as he lifted what
lay beneath the false bottom.

Medical records. A solidiograph of a smiling baby,
another, taken later, of a blond-haired, blue-eyed child
standing before a clump of trees.

The monk said, "The boy?"

"Yes. Jondelle. The medical records will give you his
physical characteristics." Dumarest studied the remaining
item. A card of flexible plastic bearing a photograph,
a name, a series of fingerprints, a list of coded symbols.
A means of identification carried by anyone who worked
in a high-security area—or a record of one which should
have remained in a file.

He looked at the face, younger than he remembered,
but no less determined.

"The woman?" The monk was curious. "The boy's
mother?"

Dumarest nodded, reading the name. "Kamar Ragnack.
She made an anagram of the first three letters of each of
the names. I don't know why, but it's obvious she was
trying to hide." He handed the papers and card to the
monk, retaining the solidiographs, turning them so as to
look at the boy from every angle. "You can copy these,"
he said. "They should help."

The monk took them, tucked them into his robe. "And
now?"

"You go back to the city and we'll be getting on with
what has to be done."

The hired raft was empty, the driver impatient to be
gone. Dumarest watched as the craft lifted, the monk
raising an arm in farewell as it carried him away. Tambolt
had landed close to stacked bales. He said, "I scanned the
area. Nothing."

"No signs of fires, ashes, torn dirt?"

"Nothing, Earl. I flew low and checked everything.
No one's been here and certainly no one is watching." He
looked at the ashes of the fires, the armored dead. "It
looks as if you had quite a time here. Did you learn
anything about the boy?"

"No."

"You wouldn't tell me if you had—but we're partners, remember?"

Dumarest looked past him to where the others sat in the body of the raft. Jasken, Preleret, four others. One, older than the rest, said, "You promised food and clothing, Earl. I'm not complaining, but it's been a long drag. When do we eat?"

His name was Sekness, a quiet man who had remained neat and clean despite his privations. He carried a short club and had lost the little finger of his right hand.

"As soon as you prepare some food." Dumarest jerked his head toward the house. "Get into the kitchen. There's food in the store and meat in the freezer." To one of the others he said, "Help him. Jasken, how's the raft?"

"Not too good." The squat man scowled and rubbed his hand along the edge of his jaw. "The engine's no problem, but the conducting strips aren't what they should be. We're low on lift. I'd guess that we're operating at about sixty percent efficiency. We can carry the men or the load, but not both."

"That's fine," snapped Tambolt. "We're beaten before we start. A hell of an engineer you turned out to be!"

"I fitted the engine," said Jasken stolidly. "Find me new conducting strips and I'll have it as good as new, but even then you'd be in trouble. The raft isn't big enough for what you want. Those bales are heavy and we're talking about eight men. Add it all up and you've got too big a load."

"We'll manage," said Dumarest.

"How?" Tambolt was savage. "I told you the money wasn't enough. "Damn it, man, have you any idea of what lies ahead? Rough ground most of the way, chasms, mountains, patches of forest. And don't think it's like what we've already covered. Past the Relad the terrain alters. I warned you it wouldn't be easy."

"If it was, I wouldn't need you," said Dumarest evenly. "Or a raft, the goods, the men. I'd have gone alone. Now stop complaining and get the bales loaded. Preleret, come with me."

In the house he jerked open a wardrobe and gestured to the clothes inside. Elray's clothes.

"Help yourself. Take what you need and share the rest among the others. Can you use a rifle?"

"If I have to, yes."

"Carry this." Dumarest handed him one of the two weapons the house contained. "There's cartridges in the drawer; make sure they are all loaded on the raft. Touch nothing and make sure that no one takes what isn't theirs. You understand?"

Preleret nodded.

"How's your woman?"

"Fine. The medics said that I got her to the infirmary just in time. She's going to be all right. They even said they might find her a job, nothing much, just doing the dirty work, but it'll provide food and shelter until I get back."

"You'll get back."

"I intend to." The man hesitated. "Earl, I'm not good at saying things. You know? But—"

"Get your clothes," said Dumarest. "And keep that gun handy. I might need you to use it sometime. You follow me?"

"Sure, Earl." Preleret drew a deep breath. "You don't want thanks and I'm not good at giving them. But I'll pay you back in some way. Don't worry—you can rely on me."

Dumarest nodded and left the house. Oustide Tambolt was supervising the loading, Jasken adjusting the bales so as to trim the raft. He glanced up as Dumarest passed, seemed about to say something, then changed his mind. The sprawled shape of an armored figure rested to one side; Dumarest passed it, halted where small craters pocked the ground, ash filling their bottoms and rounding the jagged rims. He stooped and picked up the lance he had used. A missile had struck the shaft and he looked at the ripped metal, the savage blade with its crusted point. His eyes lifted to where Makgar had lain, rose again to stare in the direction the raft had taken.

It meant nothing. They could have turned, circled, taken any direction once out of sight. The air held no traces and, even if it had, the wind would have blown them away. As it had blown the ash, the scars of the battle.

From behind Tambolt said, "Dreaming, Earl?"

"Thinking."

"About the raft? It won't carry the load and us too. We could drop some of the stuff and leave some of the men behind. Or we could take it all and leave them all.

I don't like either solution. We need the goods and we're going to need the men."

"And food," said Dumarest.

"More weight, but you're right. Men have to eat. Damn it, Earl. What can we do?"

"Use ropes. Twenty-foot lengths tied to the raft and hanging over the edge. Tie loops at the ends and we'll settle them under our arms. The raft will lift and we'll follow it. With the lift and the forward movement, we should be able to cover ten or twenty feet at a bound. Simple."

"Simple," agreed Tambolt. "On flat, soft ground and with a steady hand at the controls. But what about when the ground gets rough and there are crosswinds? The men won't like it."

"They'll like it," said Dumarest grimly. "Or they can lump it. But one thing is certain; they aren't going to quit. Once we start, we keep going until the end."

"Until we reach Melevgan."

"Until we find the boy," Dumarest corrected. He looked at the broken lance in his hand and flung it so that it stuck in the dirt. "Until we find those who took him. Now let's go and eat."

CHAPTER

TEN

The first day they covered a hundred miles, running behind and under the raft, loops tight under their armpits, slack in their hands, a hopping, bounding journey which left everyone but Dumarest and Jasken exhausted. At night they camped, eating the first big meal of the day, high-protein food, low in bulk but high in energy.

Tambolt stared at the lance Dumarest held out to him. "What's this for?"

"We're standing guard." The lance was one of four salvaged from the farm, reloaded from the goods they carried. "You, me, and Jasken. We'll overlap the shifts, two on and one off."

"I can't. I'm beat."

"You can," said Dumarest grimly. "And you will."

"The others——"

"Haven't the strength." Dumarest thrust the lance into Tambolt's hands. "All you have to do it to keep your eyes open. You see anything, you yell. If it comes at you, give it the point. If we're attacked, fire the missiles. There's nothing to it."

At dawn one of the men complained of his ankle. It was swollen, tender to the touch. Dumarest ripped up a shirt and bound it tightly, then fashioned splints with a crossbar to take the strain. Wincing, the man rose, testing it.

"I can't do it. I'll have to ride."

"You'll travel like the rest. Nurse the ankle and use the other foot—and this time be more damn careful."

The man was stubborn. "I ride or I quit. Leave me some food and one of the lances and I'll make my own way back."

"You don't ride and you don't quit," said Dumarest. "You're coming, if we have to drag you. Now get in that rope and remember what I told you. Hurt the other ankle and I'll leave you behind to rot. Now move!"

They made less progress that day, more the day after.
The ground became rough, great boulders and swaths of
jagged stone slowing them down almost to a crawl. A patch
of forest had to be circumnavigated and hills climbed. By
the time they reached the mountains the men were fit, hard
and as agile as cats. But they had reached the end of the
line.

"We're low on food," reported Sekness. "Enough for
a couple of big meals or a half dozen small ones." He
looked at the mountains soaring before them. "There
could be game up there, but I doubt it. There'd be nothing
for it to live on."

"There's no game." Tambolt was emphatic. "But
Melevgan lies over the other side. If this damn raft was
as it should be, we could get there in a day."

Jasken said, "There's nothing wrong with the raft. I'm
getting tired of you whining about it."

"You're riding all the time," snapped Tambolt. "Try
swinging on one of those damn ropes for a change and
see how you like it."

The engineer shrugged. "Each to their own skill, mister.
You think it easy handling this thing, then you try it.
I've got to guard against crosswinds, updrafts, dips, and
crests. To go fast when I can and to slow as I drop. If
I misjudge, you'd fall, get dragged, and maybe break
a few bones."

Dumarest said, "Sekness, prepare a meal, a big one.
Tambolt, Preleret, get the others and unload the raft."

"Here?" Tambolt frowned. "What's the point, Earl?
We've got to get the stuff over the mountains, not leave it
here."

"I'm going to scout the ground," said Dumarest patiently. "We might need all the lift we can get. Now
let's not waste any more time arguing about it. I want to
get it done before dark."

Unloaded, the raft lifted easily beneath Jasken's hands.
He sent it upward and toward the soaring barrier with
Dumarest at his side studying the ground below. A defile
wound, climbing and relatively smooth. It ended in a
blind canyon beyond which lay a mass of jagged stone
slashed with deep crevasses. Higher lay sheer falls, ledges
which led nowhere, overhanging cliffs, and slopes of loose
debris. The stone, harsh, blue-tinted in the emerald light,

was dotted with sparse shrubs, spined and thorny growths and hooked vines covered with savage burrs.

Jasken said, "No one could climb up that. Nor down either. I'll try farther along."

It was the same. To either side the mountains presented an impassable barrier to men on foot. Jasken swore as the raft jerked beneath them, falling to rise again with a scrape of metal against stone.

"Thermals," he said. "We're too close. There are updrafts and pockets, side winds too. You seen enough, Earl?"

"Go back to the camp and try again. Head straight for the summit."

There was a place a third of the way up, a pocket in the side of the mountain, edged by stone and invisible from below. The interior was fairly smooth, dotted with minor boulders but with enough room to land. Higher there was another and the summit was bare. Jasken grunted as the raft veered to the impact of wind.

"You want me to go over?"

"No, turn back. If anyone's down there, I don't want them to see us."

"Not sure of the reception?"

"That's right. Have you marked those areas we found or do you want to take another look?"

"I know where they are. You thinking of shifting the load a piece at a time?"

Dumarest nodded; it was the only way.

"We won't be able to carry much at a time. A third of the load with a single man. Four trips each time." Jasken sent the raft flying clear of the mountain as he headed back to the camp. "Why don't you head straight for the top and be done with it?"

Dumarest said dryly, "Have you met the Melevganians?"

"No."

"But you've heard about them?"

"Sure, but—"

"Would you like to be sitting on top of that mountain with goods of price and the nearest help way down at the bottom?"

"No," said Jasken thoughtfully. "I guess not. The time element's important. I hadn't thought of that. Is that why you didn't want to be spotted? But how could they climb the other side of the mountain?"

"I don't know. Maybe they couldn't, but Tambolt said they mine it. And, maybe, they could have a raft. When we meet, I want all the advantage I can get." Dumarest stared down and ahead. The sun was setting, thick shadows hiding the lower regions, the campfire a speck of brightness against the night. Too bright, an attraction for unwanted eyes. If the food was cooked, it would have to be extinguished. To Jasken he said, "No guard for you tonight. Eat and get all the sleep you can. Tomorrow, check the raft. As soon as the sun has warmed the air, we'll begin."

"That'll be close to noon," said Jasken. "I can't work in the dark and it'll take time for the sun to warm those rocks. Uneven temperature means uneasy air and we'll have to get in close. I'd say about two hours to noon. With luck we can get all the men and goods up to the top by late afternoon."

Dumarest went with the first load, riding with a third of the bundles, frowning as the raft jerked and responded sluggishly to the controls. Twice Jasken attempted to land, veering away at the last moment as rising air made the craft unstable. The third time he set it down with a gasp of relief. He looked at his hands, trembling from overstrain, then wiped the sweat from his face and neck.

"That was tough," he said. "It'll get easier from now on. Maybe I should lighten the load a little, make five trips instead of four."

"Try it," said Dumarest. "Bring a man with you on the next trip, another on the third. Then the rest of the goods and finally the rest of the men." He added, "Make sure the man is armed."

A caution born of long experience with strange places. The mountains looked barren, but the Melevganians were close and it would be stupid to take appearances for granted. Dumarest checked the area, the rifle he carried held in readiness, but found nothing alarming in the small pocket in which he and the bales stood: some openings like tiny caves about the size of a fist, a straggle of thorned vegetation, and a patch of spined scrub. He climbed the outer wall and stared down at the bleak expanse below. If the raft should crash, he would be trapped. It would be barely possible to fashion a rope and to cut footholds, blast them, even with the missiles in the

bales, but he had no food and only a little water. One
slip and he would fall to lie with broken legs or punctured
lungs. A damaged ankle, even, would mean his death.

He turned and stared up at the soaring expanse of the
mountain. One of the chain, Tambolt had said, which
ringed Melevgan. There could be a pass, somewhere, but
there was no time to find it. Only a raft could surmount
it and traders did not leave their rafts. If there were any
inside, they would not be used for raids.

He sat on one of the bales, thinking, taking small sips
of water to combat the moisture-sucking heat. The pocket
was like an oven reflecting the rays of the rising sun,
accentuating the heat with every passing moment. At mid-
day it would be like a furnace.

Jasken returned with a second load, smaller, more
easily handled. This time he landed at the first approach,
snapping at the man he carried.

"Get this stuff off, fast. Move!"

The man was the one who had injured his ankle. He
carried a lance which he let fall as he grappled with a
bale. Dumarest took another, Jasken a third. Within
minutes the raft was empty and rising for another journey.
As it fell, Altrane yelled, "The next time bring some food.
Water too. Understand?"

Dumarest said, "Get these bales stacked in a neat pile.
And pick up that lance."

"Why?" Altrane was sullen. "There's plenty of room
here; what's the use of double-handling?"

"Do it. Jasken needs all the room he can get. And
don't forget what we're carrying. If he should drop, slam
against one of these bales, you won't have a thing to worry
about. You'll be dead."

He was exaggerating, but the threat brought action.
Altrane placed the last of the bales and stood, sweating, his
tongue moistening his lower lip.

"Have you got any water? I'm parched." He took the
container Dumarest offered and drank greedily, water
falling past his chin to splash on the ground. "Thanks."

"Now the lance."

"You think I'll need this thing?" He picked it up and
reasted it against the bales so that the point stood upward,
wicked in the light. "What's going to attack us up here?
The vegetation? The rocks? You know, Earl, at times I

think you're a little too cautious for your own good. A little too careful. There's a name for it."

Dumarest said, flatly, "Tell me."

Altrane scowled, remembering the way he had been treated when he had hurt his ankle. It had healed, true, but it could have grown worse and no thanks to Dumarest that it hadn't. Tambolt would have been more understanding. He could get along with Tambolt. They would have been in and out by now, taking half the goods and men, a quick trade and a big profit. And he wouldn't have used his position to push a man around.

"Tell me," said Dumarest again. "What do they call a man who's too careful?"

"Nothing." It was easy to think of what he'd say and do if the chance arose. but, now that it had come, he wasn't too eager. To change the subject, Altrane said, "How much do you think we'll make?"

"I told you what you'll get. A High passage if we find enough, less if we don't."

"Yes, but suppose we make a lot more than a High passage all around? Tambolt was saying that there are fortunes in these mountains. Jewels to be had for the taking. We could really hit the jackpot. What then, Earl?"

"Nothing. We made a deal."

"You mean that no matter how much we find, all you're going to give us is the cost of a High passage? Hell, man, you call that fair? Tambolt was saying—"

"Tambolt talks too much," snapped Dumarest curtly. "And so do you. What's the point of arguing about something we haven't even found yet? Now keep quiet. Sound travels in mountains like these."

"So what? So who's to hear us?" Altrane was livid. "Listen. Let's get this straight. Are we going to share equally or not? I—"

"Shut up!"

"What? Now you see—"

"Shut your damned mouth!"

Dumarest tensed, listening. From somewhere above and to one side came a scrape, the bounce of a falling stone. More followed the first, a little rush of loosened debris, the rocks clattering as they jounced over the slope. He climbed the wall and looked over the edge in the direction from which the sound had come. He saw nothing aside from the blue-tinged rock, the scabrous green of the straggling vegetation. A fragment yielding beneath the impact of temperature change, perhaps? A root, slowly growing, slowly pushing until eroded stone showered in a tiny avalanche?

He looked higher up the mountain, the sun-glare catching his eyes and filling them with water. He blinked, caught the hint of movement, and heard Altrane's incredulous shout.

"Dear God! What is it?"

An armored thing, ten feet long, plated, clawed, a tail raised to show a sting. Thin legs scrabbled as it raced forward, blue-tinted to match the rocks among which it lurked, the legs hooked with barbs, sending stones rolling down the mountain. A mutated, scorpion-like creature which scented water and food.

Dumarest sprang back as it reared above the edge of the pocket. falling as his foot turned, rolling to rise as the thing lunged toward him. He sprang high, a claw snapping beneath his boot, landed on a rounded back to spring again as the tail stabbed where he had stood. It brushed his side and he felt the bruising impact through his tunic. The plastic tore and a green venom stained the mesh beneath.

"The lance, man!" he shouted. "Use the lance!"

Altrane crouched behind the bales, shaking, paralyzed with fear. He screamed as the thing touched the obstruction and rose above it, the scream rising to a shriek as a claw snapped and tore flesh from his arm. He ran, hitting Dumarest in his wild flight, trailing blood as he raced to the wall at the edge of the pocket. The thing turned, the lance falling, the shaft bending beneath the grip of a claw. Dumarest dodged, jumped to one side, and ran to where the bales lay scattered. The rifle lay beneath them. If he tried to get it, he would be dead before he could drag it free. He sprang to the top of the bales, leaped over the plated back and ran to the opposite side of the pocket to where Altrane stood, whimpering, clutching at his wounded arm.

The thing froze. It stood, almost indistinguishable from the stone, stalked eyes questing, tail raised to strike. It could scent prey and was temporarily undecided in which direction to go. Dumarest tensed, watching. If the thing moved away from the bales, he could get the rifle or the lance. The lance, he decided. It was in the open and closer to hand. The shaft was bent and the missile launcher useless, but the blade and point were still serviceable. With it, he could slash at the legs, the eyes, crippling and blinding the creature and gaining time to recover the rifle and the death it could give.

He said, "Move, Altrane. Run along the edge of the wall."

"No! I can't! It'll get me!"

"Not if you go fast enough. Make a feint, then dive the other way. I've got to get hold of that lance. Barehanded we haven't a chance."

"I can't, Earl! I can't!"

Dumarest stopped, snatched out his knife, threw it in one smooth gesture. It spun, reached the armored back just behind the eyes, and fell to ring against the stone. The plating was too hard to penetrate, as Dumarest had known it would be, but the impact stirred the creature. It spun, claws and tail uplifted, racing forward as Dumarest flung himself behind the bales. He heard the impact, the rip of tearing fabric, and felt a numbing impact against his boot. The sting had caught the heel. He jerked it away before it could strike again, rolling around the end of the scattered bales to snatch up the lance. The blade made an arc of brightness as it whined through the air, the sound of an ax hitting wood as it struck the joint of a segmented claw.

A yellow ichor welled about the blade, gushing as Dumarest tore it free to spatter on the ground. A fetid odor rose from where it lay.

"The rifle," snapped Dumarest. "Get it. Use it. Move!"

There was no time to see if Altrane obeyed. The thing had lunged forward again, legs rasping on the ground, moving at incredible speed. Dumarest backed, the lance held before him stabbing at the eyes, ducking under a sweeping claw to slash at the legs, to spring over the back as the tail slammed toward him, moving by unthinking reflex action, only his speed enabling him to survive.

It was a contest which couldn't last. Already he was tiring, the heart pounding in his chest, sweat dewing face and hands. A slip and the thing would have him, the massive claws crushing his body, driving splintered ribs into his lungs or pulping his intestines. A moment of inattention and the tail would descend like a mace on skull or shoulder, snapping the bone in arm or leg, the sting

tearing at naked flesh or penetrating his clothing. And it
was too well armored to be seriously hurt by the lance.
Too agile to be crippled to the point where it would be
helpless.

He risked a glance to where Altrane stood, numbed by
his terror, useless to help.

The eyes, he thought. It had to be the eyes. Blinded,
the creature might freeze long enough for him to reach
the rifle.

He lifted the lance, the shaft bent now at the point
where it had been crushed. Gripping the butt, he swung
it in a circle, light catching the smeared blade, air whining
as he backed. There was no time for careful aim. As the
thing darted toward him, he threw the lance, spinning, toward the stalked eyes. Almost he missed. The blade struck
one of the thick protrusions, the shaft the other, but too
low for what he had intended. Hurt, the creature halted,
backed a little, claws questing.

Dumarest moved.

He felt the rasp of chiton on his back as he raced,
stooped, beneath a claw. The thing had been stunned a
little, slow to respond, but he heard the scrape of hooked
feet on the ground as it turned, the wind from the stabbing
tail. Then the bales were before him and he dived over
the nearest, hitting the ground, rolling to throw his weight
against the one on the rifle. He rose, the muzzle spurting
flame as the creature reared above him.

He saw the bullets hit, blasting the eyes, the head,
the open jaw. Yellow ichor gushed from the holed car-
apace, sickening with its odor, and a claw fell, slamming
against his side, throwing him hard against the bales.

He fired again, aiming by instinct, seeing the joint of
the great pincher shatter beneath the impact of the missiles.
Other thunder joined his own. Preleret, standing on the
raft, white-faced, the rifle he carried tight against his
shoulder.

"Earl!" he called. "Earl!"

The creature turned, gusting air in a thin, high parody
of a scream. Dying, it threshed about the pocket of stone,
bales flying, air thrumming to the lash of its sting.
Dumarest heard a shriek, the blast of Preleret's rifle and
then, after what seemed a long time, silence.

Stiffly he rose. His side felt numb and blood ran from
his nose, the corner of his mouth. He looked at the

twitching shape, the raft, the figure of Altrane lying limp to one side. His chest was torn, his skin puffed and swollen from the poison of the sting which had taken his life.

"God!" Jasken drew in a shuddering breath. "Look at the size of that thing! Are you all right, Earl?"

He was bruised, his shoulder and ribs aching, but nothing was broken and he would survive. As Altrane would have survived, if he'd had the courage to act. Dumarest looked at the dead man, then at the dead creature.

"Get ropes on it," he ordered. "Lift and drag it clear. Dump it lower down the mountain, but leave it where it can be seen."

Preleret was shrewd. "As a warning?"

"As bait for any others that might be lurking around. I want no more surprises. If they come looking for easy meat, they'll find it in one of their own kind. We can watch, shoot if we have to, hold our fire if we don't."

Jasken said, "And the man? What about him?"

"The same."

"Well, now," said Jasken slowly. "Altrane wasn't much good, I'll admit. I guessed wrong with him. A troublemaker and greedy to boot. But to dump him, just like that? As food for things like the one that attacked you? Somehow it doesn't seem right."

"You want to take him back and show him to the others?" Dumarest shrugged as the man made no answer. "He's dead. He doesn't care what happens to him now. But if the others see him, they'll get scared. Split the load. Bring up two more on your next trip. They can see him when they get here and not before. Now move! I want to get to the summit before dark!"

CHAPTER

ELEVEN

They spent the night on a windswept plateau, the men nervous, staying awake and ready to shout the alarm at every sound. The bales and raft made a protective ring over which they stared into the star-shot night, seeing a danger in every shadow. At dawn they dropped into the valley, half the men at the first load, the goods, Dumarest staying until the last. The sun was bright as they left the foothills and began to cross cultivated ground. Fields of crops, orchards, bushes bearing a variety of fruit. Men and women worked the fields, small and dark, looking up as they passed, then returning to their duties.

"The Hegelt," said Tambolt. "Some of them must have been here when the Melevganians came and others have probably been brought in. They breed fast and make docile workers."

Dumarest looked ahead. They were pulling the raft now, the engine providing barely enough energy to lift the vehicle a few feet above the ground. It was slow progress, but safe and he wanted to give the impression that the craft was damaged. A precaution against theft or confiscation. A workable raft to the Melevganians would be a temptation they might choose not to ignore. A damaged one would be of little value.

"There!" Tambolt, at his side, lifted an arm, pointing. "You can see the city."

It was low, long, a rambling collection of buildings constructed in a dozen varieties of style. Grim blocks shouldered fabrications of sweeping curves and fluted roofs, tiered pagodas and convoluted spirals of no apparent purpose. Most had broad, external stairs, wide balconies and walks supported by stalked columns. The windows were paneled in fretted iron-work, panes of many shapes and colors, wide sheets of reflecting crystal, rounded bull's-eyes, curves and abstract shapes which followed no apparent symmetry. From peaked, flat, and rounded roofs fluttered pennons and gaudy ribbons, figures of weird beasts and inflated constructions striped and mottled in a variety of hues.

An amusement park, though Dumarest. A collection of individual designs interspersed with fountains which threw a rain of sparkling water into the air, of flower beds and patches of sward and mobiles which turned and chimed with soft tintinnabulations. A child's playground—or a city built by those with childlke whims.

A raft rose as they approached and swept toward them, settling a few yards ahead. It held men dressed in hatefully familiar armor, armed with lances which they kept leveled as the little party came to a halt. Another man, not armored, stepped from the raft and waited.

The reception committee. Tambolt dropped his rope and caught Dumarest by the arm as he stepped forward to where the man stood.

"Let me handle this, Earl. Don't forget they're crazy. A word and they'll be at your throat. The same word, spoken in a different tone at a different time, and they will give you everything they own. Logic doesn't work here. Not your sort of logic, at any rate."

Dumarest made no answer, looking instead at the unarmored Melevganian. He was tall, thin, his face painted in tiny flecks of color. His hair was dark, clubbed at the rear with a gemmed band. He wore soft shoes and pants, a wide belt above which showed the jeweled hilt of a knife, a short jacket, open in the front to reveal a painted chest. His lips were full, sensuous, his teeth cruelly pointed.

He said, "This is the land of the Melevganians. You are strangers."

"Traders," said Tambolt smoothly. "Men who have come to bring you things of interest. To offer our services and to bask in the sun of Melevgan."

"Which will never fade."

"Which will never fade," repeated Tambolt. "Have we your permission to remain?"

"And if it is refused?"

"We shall leave."

Dumarest saw the painted face convulse, the lips tighten, and one of the thin hands lift toward the knife.

He said quickly, "My lord, if we have offended, we crave your forgiveness. The sun of the elect is bright in our eyes and dulls our mind. Of course we cannot leave without your august permission. In all things we are your servants."

"You are gracious." The man relaxed, his hand falling from his waist, his thin, strident voice softening a little. "You please me. You carry goods, you say?"

"A few things of little worth—yet you may find them amusing."

"That could be so."

"If it is your wish to see them, the bales will be unpacked at your command."

"Later. The Guardians of Melevgan do not concern themselves with such things. But, later, if it is my whim, I shall inspect them."

"As you wish, my lord."

"You speak well," mused the man. "And you please me, as I have said. The elect are generous to those who do them service. Go now, to the house bearing the image of a hanging man. Food will be provided."

"My lord." Dumarest bowed. "May I have the honor of knowing to whom I speak?"

"Tars Boras. Commander of the Guardians and a noble of Melevgan. We shall meet again."

Tambolt released his breath as the man returned to his raft and was lifted away.

"You took a chance there, Earl. Asking his name like that. He could have turned against us."

"He didn't."

"But he could have. I told you to leave everything to me. I know how to handle them."

"Maybe." Jasken had overheard. "But it looked to me as if he were about to blow his top before Earl took over." He scowled after the vanishing shape of the raft. "The arrogant swine! I've met characters like him before. They think they own the galaxy because they've got wealth and power and consider everyone else to be less than dirt. Well, maybe we can teach him a lesson."

"No," said Dumarest.

"How come, Earl?"

"I don't want you thinking that way. We want something from these people. If we have to eat dirt to get it, then that's just what we'll do. Now let's find the house of the hanging man."

It was deep in the city, a squat cone with a staircase

spiraling outside to a pointed summit on which stood a
gallows and the figure of a suspended man. A wide door
admitted the raft and internal stairs led upward to a
semicircular chamber bright with rainbows from a dozen
windows glazed with tinted crystal. Other chambers opened
from the first containing baths and soft couches, a room
with a table containing smoking meats. Hegelt women
served them, silent on naked feet, shapeless beneath robes
of nondescript gray.

Tambolt said, "For these who don't know better, let
me give a warning. Don't touch the women or interfere
with them in any way. They keep to themselves and the
Melevganians won't have anything to do with them. Men
don't mate with animals and to them that's just what the
Hegelt are. If you touch them, you'll demean yourselves
and the rest of us with you. I want to get out of here
alive and rich, but at least alive. You understand?"

Preleret said, "I'm not interested in these girls. I've got
a woman back in Sargone. All I'm interested in is money."

"And there's plenty of it around," said one of the
others. "Did you see those jewels that character was
wearing? How much do you think the stuff we brought is
worth, Tambolt? Can we screw up the price, maybe?"

Greed, thought Dumarest, but it was an emotion to be
used. Had been used. He pushed aside his plate and left
the table. In the large, semicircular room he stepped to
one of the windows and tried to look outside. The tinted
panes distorted his view, imperfections in the crystal blur-
ring clear vision either by accident or design. Were all
traders arriving in Melevgan put in this house to wait the
pleasure of the elect? Was it a means to keep them from
learning too much?

To one of the Hegelt women he said, "Are we permitted
to leave?"

"Master?"

"Can we go outside?"

"There are Guardians below, master. It would not be
wise to attempt to pass them."

Prisoners, then, or guests who had to remain where
put. Dumarest tested one of the windows, remembering
the spiral staircase outside. The guards would be inside the
building watching both raft and door. Or perhaps they
stood outside the wide panels. If he could reach the external stair and drop from it, he could leave unseen.

The window seemed jammed. He moved to another, the girl padding behind him.

"Master, why do you wish to leave and go outside?"

To learn. To ask about the things he wanted to know. To discover, somehow, if the boy was in the city. Perhaps Tars Boras would tell him, but he doubted it. The man had been too ready to reach for his knife, too quick to take offense. Questions about Jondelle would only serve to drive him into a rage. A rage all the more intense if he'd had anything to do with the raid.

A third window resisted his pressure. The woman said, "Upstairs, master. If you want to see outside. There is a window which opens."

It was in a small room musty with the scent of neglect. A rumpled heap of clothing stood in a corner, plastic ripped and torn, in one place stained with something which could have been blood. Dumarest thought of the shape of the man hanging above. A real man, perhaps? One killed in a sudden rage and left to hang? Coated, maybe, with a preserving agent to provide a macabre decoration?

The window opened with a creak, a gust of cool air blowing away the odors of the room. A narrow ledge opened on an empty space. Dumarest leaned over and saw the upper limit of the spiral staircase below. It was seven feet from the window, a narrow band three feet wide winding around the outside of the building. Like a helter-skelter, he thought. If it had been smooth, he could have ridden down it on a mat.

Overhead the gallows creaked a little beneath the impact of the wind. He stared up toward it, seeing the hanging shape, the distorted grimace on the face beneath its transparent plastic film. The face was unpainted, the teeth unfiled, the skin a golden copper, the hair streaked with blond. A stranger who had said the wrong thing at the wrong time and who had paid the price.

The gallows creaked again as Dumarest eased his body through the window, to hang a second before falling to drop on the stairs.

They were greased and had no rail.

He felt his boots slip and flung out his arms as he fell. His hands hit the slimed surface, slipped as his body rolled over the edge, caught as they hit the patch wiped clean by his legs. The wind gusted between his body and the building, forcing him outward from the wall. He glanced down. The next turn of the spiral was twelve feet below and to his rear, carried outward by the expanding base of the building. He could fall and hit it, but if it were greased, his body would be thrown to one side as his boots hit the uneven surface. A second spiral lay below the first, yet more beyond that. If he fell, he would bounce from one to the other to the ground a hundred feet below.

He felt his hands begin to slip, the grease on his fingers making it impossible to hold his weight against the wind. Gritting his teeth, he clamped his fingers on the stone, pulling, the muscles in arms, back, and shoulders cracking beneath the strain. The edge drew close to his eyes, his chin. He thrust his head forward and felt stone beneath his jaw. A surge and he had his elbow on the edge of a step. Another, a knee. He paused, gasping, spreading his weight over the treacherous surface. Slowly he eased his body back onto the stairs, rolling tight against the wall. He slipped a little and halted the movement with the heel of a boot. Cautiously he rose and, as if stepping on eggs, moved slowly down the stair.

He jumped while ten feet above the ground, landing in a flower bed, rising to brush dirt from his clothing before venturing into the city.

It reminded him of Sargone, the streets all in curves and random windings. But where the city of Sargone had been built by thieves for protection, this had been constructed by random directives and distorted imagination. The curves were interspersed by zigzagging lanes of varying width, streets which looped in circles for no apparent reason, roads which ended against the blank walls of buildings. And everywhere the Hegelt with brooms to sweep and dusters to polish, crouching back as arrogant Melevganians strode past, in pairs, singly, riding on litters, or dreaming as they glided on tiny rafts suitable only to lift and carry a man at little more than a walking pace a foot above the ground.

The clothes they wore matched the buldings in the variety of their style and color. Some had painted faces and hair laced with gemmed ribbons; others wore drab smocks and tangled manes, their faces pale, introspective. Some grinned at secret amusement; others scowled with inner rage. A kaleidoscope of dress and expression, but all had the height, the fish-pallor whiteness, the hauteur which stamped them for what they were.

Dumarest felt a touch and turned to see a man standing before him. He was smeared with red and black, a rag about his loins, an elaborate headdress of feathers, gems, and trailing ribbons on his shaven skull. His hands groped before him, but he was not blind.

"There is something before me," he keened. "A solidification of the air, for my theories cannot be mistaken. Nothing can exist unless I give it permission to have being. Therefore what I touch must be an illusion. I will summon my mental powers and dissolve it, send it back to the chaos from whence it came. The purity of my mind must not be contaminated by unreal phenomena. Begone!"

Dumarest stepped aside and the man walked past, mouth wreathed in triumph.

"Thus I have yet more proof of the ascendancy of my mind. The universe exists because of my wish. Darkness and chaos comes with the closing of my eyes. All things are made by the concentration of my thoughts. Truly, I am a veritable god!"

A madman, but others were not so deluded. Dumarest felt the impact of eyes and saw a pair of Melevganians looking toward him. They were young, painted of face, aspiring Guardians, perhaps, or those similar to the ones who had raided the farm. Warrior-types enamored of the lure of combat. Dangerous.

To run would be to betray himself. Instead he strode forward to meet them, making his voice thin, keening.

"You will direct me toward the House of Control. Immediately!"

He had white skin, dark hair, the arrogant manner of a man born to command. He had the height and had adopted the hauteur. His clothing was what any of them might have chosen to wear. And he had attacked in the meaning of their culture.

"Quickly!" His hand dropped toward his knife, lifted, weighted with glistening steel. "Direct me!"

One of the men drew in his breath. "There is no such place as that you seek."

"There is. There must be. I say that it exists and so it must. Quickly, now. Direct me or pay for your disrespect!" He lifted the knife and slashed suddenly at the nearer of the two men. The point caught fabric, ripped, showed naked flesh beneath. "You!" The point lanced at the other man. "You smile! I saw you smile!"

"No! You are mistaken! I—"

The man sprang back as Dumarest sent the blade of his knife whistling through the air. The cut was deliberately short, but he couldn't know that. Couldn't know either that the grating voice was a facade.

"You dare to defy me? You offer a challenge? So be it. To the death, then. To the death!"

They ran, madmen giving respect to madness, or perhaps they were saner than he had given them credit for being. They had seen his eyes, the determination they held. Men who killed and burned and treated violence to others as a game could deserve no mercy. Had they stood, he would have marked them. Had they fought, they would have died.

A voice said, "That was pretty cool, mister. Do you hope to get away with it?"

Dumarest spun, the knife falling as he saw who had spoken. She reclined in a litter supported by four male Hegelt, kilted in scarlet with a broad sash of the same color running from left shoulder to hip. Their feet were sandaled and they stood, staring ahead as if utterly indifferent to what was going on around them.

The woman said, "Put away that knife, Earl. You won't be needing it."

"You know me?"

"I know about you," she corrected. "I know that you shouldn't have left the house and I know that those two freaks you scared won't remain that way for long. They'll be back spoiling for trouble. You could probably take care of them, but they'll have friends. If you don't want to wind up gutted and hanging from a pole, you'd better get in here."

The litter was roofed with tapestry supported on thin columns at each corner, curtains drawn back and held by scarlet cords. It dipped a little as Dumarest spread his length on the cushions, rising with a soft hum as the anti-grav generator compensated for the extra weight. The Hegelt didn't have to carry the burden, only pull it and steady its progress.

"Home," ordered the woman and, as they began to trot forward, released the scarlet cords and allowed the curtains to fall. Leaning back she said, "Earl Dumarest. A nice name. I like it. Welcome to Melevgan, Earl—but what the hell took you so long?"

CHAPTER

TWELVE

She was long and slim with a ripe maturity which had fleshed her bones so that the sweep of thigh and calf matched the swell of hips and breasts. She wore a wide belt of crimson leather studded with gems, pantaloons of some diaphanous material, softly yellow, caught at the ankles and slit so as to reveal the flesh beneath. Her torso was bare aside from a short jacket, open at the front and cut high above the waist. Beneath it her breasts, high, proud, showed their soft rotundity. Her skin was a golden copper traced with curvilinear lines of vivid blue. Her eyes were painted, crusted with sparkling fragments on the upper lids, the brows thin and arched like a drawn bow. The hair, loose around her shoulders, was copper touched with blonde, dusted with sparkle to match her eyes.

Dumarest watched as she smiled, the full lips parting to show broad, white teeth. He thought of the hanging man he had seen. Was she a member of the same race? She was certainly not a Melevganian.

He said, cautiously, "You were expecting me?"

"You or someone like you. Didn't—" She broke off her eyes cautious. "My name is Neema. Doesn't it mean anything to you?"

"No."

"Then—" She broke off again, shrugging, her breast lifting beneath the jacket. "A coincidence; well, they happen. Let's just say that I was expecting someone. I thought you were him. Apparently you're not. So what brought you to Melevgan?"

"You know that," he said. "If you know my name, you must know why I'm here."

"To trade—or so your partner told me. I've been to the house. When you couldn't be found, I came looking for you. It's lucky that I did. How long did you think you could last wandering around the city on your own?"

They were lying very close, side by side in the soft crimson light within the litter, his head a little above her own so that as she looked up at him he could see the sharp triangulation of her jaw. Her smile reminded him of a cat. Her perfume of a field of flowers on a sultry summer's day.

"You're a strong man, Earl, and in any other city you'd have no trouble getting by. But this isn't a normal city. The Melevganians are insane; didn't you know that? They don't like strangers. You may have got away with it with the pair you faced down, but there would be others, and one of them could have recognized you for what you are. A hunt would have started with you as the quarry. Have you ever been chased by a mob? It isn't pleasant. I've seen it happen and I never want to see it again. The noise—like slavering dogs. The end—they like to hear a man scream."

And then they'd take him, thought Dumarest grimly, and hang him on a building for use as an ornament. Yet the woman was a stranger. He said so and she shrugged.

"I'm tolerated. Accepted even. I came here five years ago and was lucky enough to be able to treat one of the nobles. He'd gone into psychic shock and was running amok. It was either kill him or calm him down. I had some drugs and managed to get close enough to blast them into his hide. When he recovered he gave me a house, servants, the freedom of the city. I've been tolerated ever since." She drew in her breath. "The man I was with wasn't so lucky."

"Are you a doctor?"

"I've trained in psychiatry. I knew what things were like here and made preparations. Two years in a mental ward learning how to handle the insane, studying at night, saving every penny in order to get the equipment—" She broke off and then said, flatly, "We should have stayed in Urmile."

"Your home?"

"Yes. A small, restricted town with established families and a stagnant culture. I'd moved around . . . Frome, Ikinold, Sargone . . . and I guess I got restless. With money you can travel the galaxy; without it you spend your life in a trap. So I went back home and worked to hit the jackpot. Melevgan is rich. If you can survive here, you've got it made."

Greed, the most potent force in the universe, the drive which made men risk their very lives. Dumarest looked at the woman, seeing the thin lines which traced a path beneath the paint on her face, the shadows which ran from nose to mouth. She had seemed young but mature; now he knew that she was older than he had first guessed.

He said, "And do you like it here?"

"Living among a load of nuts? What do you think?" Her laughter was brittle, devoid of humor. "Can you even begin to imagine what it's like? I'm tolerated, sure, but at any moment one of these painted freaks might decide to find out what I look like inside. Every moment of every day I live balanced on the edge of a volcano. I have to pander to them, guide them, eat dirt, and talk smooth. If it wasn't for some of the more stable members of the nobility, I wouldn't be able to do it. They're crazy by our standards, but sane when compared to the rest. And I have my defenses."

She lifted her left hand and Dumarest saw the heavy bracelet, the thin tube extending from a web of filigree which extended over the back of her hand.

"A dart gun. I wear a pair of them. If any of the Melevganians gets too way out I put him to sleep. One day I'll miss or the guns won't work or there'll be just too many of them. It's only a matter of time."

She rose as the litter slowed, drawing aside the curtains as it came to a halt. Ahead the street was blocked by a mass of people. From the crowd rose a thin keening and Dumarest felt his nerves twitch as to the scratching of a nail on slate.

"Langed! What is wrong?"

The Hegelt on the front right-hand side of the litter spoke without turning his head.

"The way is blocked, my lady."

"Then turn around. Go back and find another route. Quickly!"

She dropped the curtains as the litter began to turn. Her face was strained, anxious.

"The fools!" she stormed. "The dumb, ignorant, stupid fools!"

"The Hegelt?"

"Yes." She caught his hand as Dumarest made to draw back the curtain. "Don't look. Don't let them see you. A crowd like that means trouble. Mass hysteria building to break out in a wave of violence—and those damn fools headed straight toward it."

He looked at her hand where it gripped his own. It was trembling. Gently Dumarest disengaged her fingers.

"Why?" he said. "Why should they do that?"

"The Hegelt? Who knows? They could be the ones to get it, but they never seem to care. Or perhaps they wanted to put me in danger." She scowled, suddenly ugly. "They don't like me. No one in the entire city likes me. They're jealous of what I've got and what I am. Everytime I go out I can feel them watching me. Earl! I—"

Abruptly she broke into a storm of weeping, her hands clinging to his shoulders, the nails digging into the plastic of his tunic. He held her close, soothing, his face bleak as he looked past the shimmering glory of her hair. A woman with more greed than sense or perhaps one whose greed had led her into a trap. Contaminated by the insanity among which she lived, the twisted logic of those around her warping her own mental processes, eroding the emotional restraints common to a normal mind, giving her a paranoid complex.

Or perhaps she was a woman in an extremity of fear who had reason to be terrified and who had succumbed to emotion when it could no longer be contained.

Raising his voice Dumarest said, "Langed! Take the shortest route to your mistress' home. If you see a crowd, avoid it."

"Yes, master."

"And hurry."

Neema had regained her self-control by the time they arrived at a domed structure striped with swirls of red and yellow and vivid blue. Dumarest followed her inside to a small chamber softly feminine with subdued light nacreous through windows of shimmering pearl. A Melevganian stood waiting, tall, his face a psychedelic nightmare. His robe was of a dull orange and fell from shoulders to floor in an unbroken line.

He said, curtly, "I am told that the goods the traders brought have been purchased by you."

Neema bowed, her voice soft. "That is so, my lord."

"I want them."

"Then they are yours, my lord."

"And if I do not choose to pay?"

"They are yours, my lord," she repeated. "Mine will be the honor of serving the elect."

The nightmare face opened to show filed teeth.

"You speak well, Neema. It pleases me to take them. The Guardians need the missiles the bales contain for the protection of the city and thus the protection of yourself. And there are other things of value. Our equipment at the mines lacks efficiency, but that can now be remedied. You have done well."

"Your words are a kindness, my lord," said Neema. "May I be so bold as to ask after your son?"

"He does well."

"And his sleep?"

"No longer does he wake the house with screaming. Your potions have worked their magic. You will send more to my house before it is dark." The tall figure threw a bag to the floor. It fell on the carpet with a rattle of stones. "For the potions."

"You are most generous, my lord."

"It pleases me to be so. Farewell!"

Dumarest stooped and picked up the bag as the man left. Not once had the eyes in the painted face looked at him; to the Melevganian he had simply not existed. Opening the pouch, he looked at the mass of gems. His expenses, back; a High passage for each of the men who had accompanied him; more.

But the bag was empty of the one thing he wanted.

To Neema he said, quietly, "You jumped the gun. Those goods weren't yours to sell."

"No?" She met his eyes. "Think again, Earl. Your partner sold them to me for half of what you hold."

Tambolt eager for a quick profit and a safe skin. It was like the man to act without thinking and yet surely he could not have been so naïve as to have taken the first offer. Dumarest held back the gems as she reached for them.

"You have that in writing?"

"Don't be a fool. Of course not." She sighed at his expression. "I was working on commission. Fifty percent of what I could get. I know the market, you don't. I know how to get the money, you don't. You heard Tars Qualelle. He just took the goods and would have taken your life too had you protested. I had to con him. That money is for the drugs I supply to keep his idiot son quiet at night. It's the only way to do business here in Melevgan.

I've had five years' practice. Don't you think I deserve a commission?"

"Fifty percent?"

"Twenty-five then. Damn it, Earl, what's the matter? Isn't the money enough for you?"

"I wanted more than money. I wanted information."

She listened as he told her about the boy and why he had come to Melevgan. Crossing to a cabinet, she produced wine and filled two glasses. As she sipped, her eyes met his, very direct, calculating even.

"This boy—Jondelle—is he worth anything to you?"

"In money? No."

"Then why are you concerned about him? No," she added before he could answer. "Don't bother to tell me. If you don't want to cash in on him, then there's only one reason. You like him. You made a promise and you're going to keep it. Fair enough. But he isn't in Melevgan."

"Are you sure about that?"

"I'm sure." She sipped again at her wine. "What's it worth to me if I help you?"

Dumarest hefted the bag of gems, the stones emitting a harsh rattle.

"Not that. Not money. I need help. If I help you, will you help me in return?"

"If I can, yes."

"You're cautious," she said. "I like that. You don't promise what you can't give, but once you give your word that's it. I'll tell you what I want. I want to get the hell away from here. From Melevgan and all the nuts around me. I want to be able to see a man without wondering if he's going to shove a knife in my side as I pass. To be able to entertain friends for dinner, to walk unarmed, to look a man in the eye and tell him what I think instead of having to crawl and eat dirt. I want to escape."

She paused, breathing deeply, her breasts prominent beneath the jacket. She looked at the goblet in her hand and abruptly swallowed what it contained, glass rattling as she refilled it from the bottle.

"I want to escape," she said again. "Dear God, Earl! You can't guess how much I want to escape."

"Take a raft and go," said Dumarest flatly. "It's as simple as that."

"You think so?" Her shrug was eloquent. "The only rafts with enough lift to pass the mountains are held by the Guardians. The rest are toys, powerful only enough to drift. They can't be adapted. The only free raft in the place is the one you came with. The only way I can get out as if you take me. You, your raft, your men to give protection."

"The raft is damaged," lied Dumarest. "It burned out on the way down."

"Then you're in trouble." Again she emptied her glass. "The mountains can't be climbed and the Guardians won't help to lift you over. Get it repaired or you'll stay here for life. It won't be a long life," she added. "And it won't be an easy one. Traders are tolerated to a certain extent because the Melevganians need the things they bring. But they've got no patience. Start moving soon or you won't be able to move at all. You'll be too damn busy to do more than sweat and breathe. Can the raft be repaired?"

Dumarest was noncommittal. "Perhaps."

"I'm rich," said Neema. "I've been here five years and I haven't wasted my time. Get me to Sargone, Earl, and I'll double what you hold in your hand. Is it a deal?"

"If I can get you out, I will."

"Your word?" She smiled as he nodded, relaxing as she helped herself to yet more wine. "Now, maybe, I can sleep tonight." She glanced at him, her eyes suggestive. "Earl?"

"The boy," he said. "Tell me what you know about him."

"About the boy, nothing. About the men who took him, not much more. Four of them arrived here a short while ago, about two days before you said the boy was taken. They had a raft and some goods and traded at profit. One was a very big man, Euluch. Heeg Euluch. heard one of the others call him that. He collected few wild aspirants to Guardianship and left. That's all know."

Dumarest looked at the bag in his hands. He dropped it and crossed the space between himself and the woman in three long strides. Gripping her shoulders he said, harshly, "That isn't enough, woman! Tell me more!"

She winced, pulling at his wrists.

"Earl! You're hurting me!"

"Talk, damn you!"

For a moment their eyes met and then his hands moved, knocking aside the tubes aimed at his face. Tightly he said, "Use those things on me and I'll break both your arms. You want to leave here, Neema? All right. I'll take you. But first you've got to tell me what I want to know. Where is Jondelle?"

"The boy? I don't know."

"But the men who took him. You know more than what you've told me. Where did they come from? What did they look like?"

"Like men," she said, sullenly. "Euluch was a giant, the others normal. They had yellow skins."

"Charnians?"

"They could have been. They grow them like that in the Valley, but people get around, Earl. They could have come from anywhere on Ourelle."

Or off of it, he thought grimly. But to start thinking that was to compound the difficulties of the situation. He had to work on the assumption that the boy was still on this world and those who took him a part of it.

"Those who went with Euluch," he said. "The Melevganians. One was named Tars Krandle. Could he have been a relative of Tars Boras or that other one, Tars Qualelle? Is Tars a family name?"

"Yes," she said. "But it's also a title. Something like 'champion,' or 'defender.' Every Guardian is called Tars something or other, but the relationship is so weak as to be almost meaningless. Inbreeding," she explained. "The son takes the title of his mother, the husband his wife. About a quarter of the population is of the Tars family and all of them are Guardians. Then we have the Yelm; they concentrate on agriculture and the food supply. Then there is the Aruk; they—"

"Never mind," snapped Dumarest. He was in no mood to learn about the Melevganian culture. "Would anyone be worrying about him or the others who died?"

"No," said Neema. "Not now. Short memories," she explained. "And no Melevganian gives a damn about another once he's grown."

"So a stranger arrived here on a raft and traded some goods," said Dumarest slowly. "Then he asked for a few volunteers to help him to steal a boy. Offered money and a night of fun if they would agree. But how could they have trusted him? He could have been a slaver or someone after a few specimens for a zoo. How did they know he would bring them back when the job was done? A man willing to kill in order to steal a boy wouldn't have stopped at cutting them down to rid himself of an inconvenience. The Melevganians may be crazy, but they aren't complete fools. They would have safeguarded themselves in some way. How, Neema? How did they do it?"

Slowly she poured herself more wine, drank, and looked thoughtfully at the goblet.

"Neema?"

"You're hard, Earl," she said. "Hard and shrewd. I wasn't going to tell you this because—well, never mind. You won't stop until you get the answer. Four men arrived on that raft. I made Euluch the same proposition I made you, but he didn't want to know. He was busy, he said, and had no time to rescue a stupid woman. Now I know what he had in mind."

Dumarest said, quietly, "And?"

"Four men arrived on the raft, but only two left with the Melevganians. The others were kept behind as hostages." Neema lifted her glass and drank it empty. When she lowered it her, full lips glistened with moisture. "They're still here. Chained and working in the mines. Sweating themselves to death as you will be—unless you can mend your raft."

CHAPTER

THIRTEEN

Jasken said, "I don't like it, Earl. I don't like it one little bit."

He turned and looked back the way they had come, at the raft which had brought them, floating now a hundred feet from the opening where they stood, armored men casual as they lounged in the body of the vehicle. He stepped to the edge and looked down at the side of the mountain. Stone fell sheer from where he stood, rose above in an unbroken wall. He turned again, scowling, shaking his head as he rejoined Dumarest.

"A hell of a place for a mine," he grumbled. "What happens if there's a fall? How do we get out if they decide to leave us here?"

"They won't," said Dumarest. "You're an expert on mining equipment. You've agreed to check some of the machines and to see what can be done about repairs. Before you can fix them, you'll have to return to the city and I must go with you. They value the machines more than a couple of potential slaves."

Jasken grunted, unconvinced. A plume of dust fell from overhead followed almost immediately after by a dull concussion.

"The crazy fools are blasting!" Jasken glared at the Melevganian who stood with another to one side. All wore thick coveralls of dusty scarlet. Their faces bore whorls of granular paint. The Geth, those who were in hereditary charge of the mines.

One of them came forward and said, "We are ready for you to begin."

A command loaded with the arrogance which was natural to Melevgan, but tempered by hard experience and brutal fact. Rocks did not leap to obey and stone cared nothing for titles and self-delusion. Of all the Melevganians the Geth were the most sane.

Dumarest said, "My companion will study your machinery to see what needs to be done. I will examine the mine to evaluate matters of priority." He added, "With your permission, naturally, my lord."

Geth Iema frowned. "I do not understand."

"It is not enough to increase the efficiency of, say, a drill," explained Dumarest. "Of what use to fill the air with dust when there is no means of ventilation to carry it away? The workers will choke and die and production slowed to a point lower than it was before. No, before we can make the best of the machinery available a survey will have to be made."

The overseer blinked, struggling with unfamiliar logic. Slaves were slaves. If they died, they could be replaced.

"It will not take long, my lord," said Dumarest quickly. "And there is no need to concern yourself. I can manage alone."

From somewhere down the tunnel a high-pitched scream rose to break with a screech of metal. A unit, overloaded, burned out and perhaps damaged beyond repair. Geth Iema made up his mind.

"You will do what needs to be done," he ordered. "I shall wait for you here. You will touch nothing but the machinery, talk to no one but the overseers. Go!"

The tunnel was long, winding, thick with dust which hung like a pale mist in the air. Galleries opened from it and lights showed yellow in the gloom. Jasken halted, wet a finger, and held it high above his head.

"No ventilation to speak of," he said. "These tunnels must branch for miles to either side. How the hell do they manage to breathe without pumps and fans?" He reached out and touched a support. Dust showered as he shook it. "Rotten. The timber's just a shell over leached wood. It needs replacing. Every damned support in the place needs replacing. If we had any sense, Earl, we'd get out of here."

"Later," said Dumarest. "After I've found out what I came for."

"You think you can find those men?" Jasken shrugged. "Two men among all the rest? Well, I agreed to play along and that's just what I'll do. I'm only hoping that Tambolt doesn't take it into his head to leave us behind."

"He can't."

"What's to stop him? The woman won't care who she pays as long as she gets away and Tambolt won't care who he leaves behind as long as he makes his profit. Maybe you're trusting him too much, Earl."

"He can't leave," said Dumarest patiently. "I've got a part of the engine. He can't use the raft until he gets it."

Insurance, he though. A precaution as leaving Preleret in charge had been a precaution. A man could be overpowered, killed even, and a part found if given time enough, but both should give all the protection needed. And if anyone was curious about the raft, its failure to operate would back his lie.

He said, "Let's get deeper into the mine. I want to find where the men are working. You can check any machinery in sight and provide a distraction if one is needed. Now let's get on with it."

Grumbling, Jasken obeyed. The mine twitched at his nerves, filling him with foreboding. The tunnels were too narrow, the dust too thick, and the supports worried him. Falls, in such a place, would be common. There was little danger of damp in a mine so high, and the rock would not burn and thus offer the danger of explosion, but every mine had its dangers and he could scent them like a dog.

Ahead, the tunnel widened, branched, lights showing the way to a gallery and a narrow face. The crack of whips echoed thinly through the air, followed by a rumble and a thin scream. Dust billowed, catching at throat and lungs. From somewhere a machine hummed with a strident irregularity.

It crouched like a monster against a wall, steel claws ripping at the stone, sending it showering back to where men crouched sorting through the debris. Other men humped the discarded rubble to where a fissure gaped in the floor. From it rose a stream of air, dry, acrid. A vent to a lower cavern, Dumarest guessed. An underground chamber which must open somewhere to the outer air.

He looked at the workers . . . slaves, collared and chained with flexible links to a stake driven into the wall. Over them stood Melevganians similar to the ones he had seen when entering the mine. They stood, arrogant, whips in their hands, sending the lash at random intervals at the naked bodies of the crouching men. From time to time one of the workers would rise, bowing, handing a stone to one of the overseers.

For reward he was given a cup of water and a thin slice of concentrates.

A nice system, thought Dumarest savagely. The men worked or they were whipped. They found gems or they starved. He caught Jasken's arm as the man stepped forward, his face ugly.

"Hold it!"

"But, Earl! Those men! Look at the swine lash at their backs."

"We can't alter it, so we must accept it," snapped Dumarest. "And we didn't come here to get ourselves killed. Try anything and you'll wind up with a chain around your neck." He pointed over to the other side of the gallery where a machine stood unattended and silent. "See what's wrong with that. Make some noise. I'm going to look around."

He stepped forward, bowing to the overseers who stared at him with incurious eyes. He was unchained and so could not be a slave. He was here so must have been accepted and passed by the outer guards. Therefore he could be ignored.

In a patch of shadow he dropped and said to a sweating man, "I'm looking for someone. He hasn't been here long and would have a friend. A man with a yellow skin. Have you seen him?"

Pale eyes glared at him from a haggard face. "Don't stop me working, mister. I can't take much more of the whip and I haven't eaten all day. Don't stop me working!"

Dumarest passed on. Men were busy slamming heavy bars against the stone, others dragging at lumps of rock loosened by hammered wedges. Noise and dust were everywhere. Men gasped, dived for a stone, fought over it as dogs over a bone, the winner going to collect his reward.

Food, water, a chance to live.

A whistle shrilled and work ceased, slaves passing down the gallery with buckets of water, handing a cup to each man. Dumarest watched as Jasken busied himself with the machine, metallic bangings coming from where he worked. There were no Hegelt; the small, dark men probably died as soon as impressed. There were tall men with slanted eyes, others with ebon skins powdered with sandy dust, some with white and olive. None he could see with yellow. The Charnians must be elsewhere.

He found one at the end of a low gallery, bent double

as he drove a short pick into the stone. The smooth skin was blemished with scars and welts, ugly bruises and scrapes which oozed blood under the dust. He jumped as Dumarest touched him, cringing, one arm lifted as if to ward off a blow.

"What's your name?" Dumarest asked.

The Charnian looked up suspiciously, but the hard eyes meeting his forced an answer. "Sheem. Why do you want to know?"

"I've been looking for you, Sheem. . . . Heeg Euluch," said Dumarest. "Tell me about him."

"Are you his friend?" Hope shone in the bloodshot eyes. "Has he returned? I knew that he wouldn't let me down. When did he arive? How soon can I get out of here?"

"He's no friend," said Dumarest harshly. "He hasn't come back. He's living it high somewhere while you rot in this stinking mine. Think of it," he urged. "A nice place with a woman, maybe. Some wine, cool, in goblets wet with condensation. Soft food of a dozen different flavors. Decent air to breathe and maybe a gentle wind to carry the scent of flowers. Why should he worry about you?"

The man looked at the pick in his hand, the knuckles taut beneath the skin.

"The pig," he said thickly. "The stinking pig."

"He used you," said Dumarest. "He got you to help him do a job and then he dumped you. A nice man. Your friend? With a friend like that, who needs enemies?"

The man shook his head, unbelieving. "He wouldn't. He couldn't."

"He did. Do you think all this is a dream?" Dumarest gestured around the shaft, the heaps of debris. "He left you as a hostage and he knew damn well what would happen to you if he didn't come back. Where did you meet him?"

"In the Valley. Me and Famur grew up together and wanted to spread our wings. We met up with Euluch and did a few things together. Then this job came along."

Dumarest said, "What was the name of the other man, the one who went with Euluch?"

"Urlat, Chen Urlat."

"From?"

"I don't know. He was with Euluch when we joined up with him." The man blinked and swallowed. "Listen, mister. Can you buy me out of here? I'll do anything if you'll get me free. Please, mister. Please!"

"There were two of you. Where's the other one?"

"Famur? He's dead. A rock fall caught him the second day they threw us in here. You'll get me out, mister? Please!"

A whip cracked sharply and the man screamed as the lash curled about his shoulders. An overseer stood, stooped in the gallery, the whip lifted for a second blow. Dumarest rose, turning so the lash missed him, bowing to hide the hate in his eyes.

"My lord?"

"You must not talk to the slaves. When they talk, they do not work. If you stop them working, then you will join them."

"I hear and obey, my lord." Dumarest fought the inclination to grab the whip, to send the lash across the arrogant face, to smash the painted visage with the heavy butt. "But I was examining the rock. The tool the man is using is not the best for the work at hand. If the haft was longer and the head less wide, a greater efficiency would be obtained. With your gracious permission, my lord, I will continue my studies."

"You will not talk?"

"How could I disobey the instructions of the elect, my lord? As you command, so it will be."

The Melevganian nodded, arrogance blinding him to the ambiguity of the reply, but making no effort to move away from where he stood. From where Jasken stood by the machine came a sudden whine of energy, the shrill of an unloaded drive. His yell of triumph rose above the sound.

"Got it! Now if someone could get me a drill?"

The overseer turned, his attention caught by the distraction, and Dumarest stooped, his voice low.

"Quickly, now. Where did Euluch intend taking the boy?"

"I don't know. He didn't say."

"But you knew what he was after?"

The man shrugged. "Sure. A kidnap job for a fat payoff. A pity it was a bust."

"It was no bust," said Dumarest harshly. "And Euluch knew exactly what he was doing. Some Melevganians to do the dirty work and a couple of fools to use as hostages. You and Famur. Your friend is dead and you could follow.

If you got out of here, where would you look for Euluch?"

"You going to get me out?"

"Maybe . . . now talk."

From somewhere along the gallery came the crack of a whip followed by a scream of pain. The sound killed the Charnian's hesitation. "In the Valley. There's a tavern, the Sumba. I'd look for him there." His hand reached out and caught Dumarest by the arm. "And now, mister, for God's sake! Get me out of here!"

Dumarest shook off the hand and rose, his eyes bleak. No man should be chained like an animal and forced to work as a slave. But he had no pity for anyone who had agreed to steal a child.

"You're a man," he snapped. "Get yourself out. You've got tools which could be used as weapons. There's a fissure in the mine which must lead to the outside. Talk to a few others, kill the overseers, and make a break for it."

"I can't! They'd kill me!"

"Yes," said Dumarest flatly. "If you don't make it, they'll kill you. But they're going to do that anyway, so what can you lose?"

CHAPTER
FOURTEEN

It was late when they left the mine, the emerald sun low over the mountains, casting broad swaths of shadow from the jagged summits over the foothills and cultivated ground. Jasken sat next to Dumarest in the body of the raft, uneasy because of the armored figures which sat like statues at front and rear. His voice was low, anxious.

"I didn't think they'd let us out, Earl. That overseer, Geth Iema, was pretty definite."

"He liked the way you fixed that machine," said Dumarest. "You impressed him. Maybe you should think about taking his offer. A house, servants, jewels, and soft living. All you have to do is to keep the mine equipment functioning."

"And if one day I can't?" Jasken shuddered. "Did you see those poor devils? Chained and beaten and breathing that stinking dust? One slip and they'll have me among them. One wrong word to an overseer even would do it." He glowered at the armored figures ahead. "They like their own way, these people. Geth Iema didn't want to let us go."

It had taken smooth talk, lies, and extravagant promises, but Dumarest knew they were not yet in the clear. Out of the mine, perhaps, but Melevgan was a prison in itself. And the longer they waited, the more dangerous it became. Jasken was of value to the Melevganians, himself and the others easily available labor for the mines.

Loudly he said, "I think you should take the offer. With the things we brought with us you could do quite a few of the needed repairs. And I can bring in anything you need. Tambolt and a couple of the others can stay as hostages and maybe we could build up a real service between here and Sargone." He added, for the benefit of listening ears, "And it would be an honor to serve the elect. Even to be close to them gives a man a sense of pride."

Jasken turned, his eyes incredulous. "Earl! What the

hell's got in—" He broke off as an elbow jabbed his ribs.

"You agree it's a good idea, Jasken?" Dumarest kept his voice loud. "Think of it, man. A fine house and all you could ever hope to gain. You know the work, for you it would be easy, and we can arrange to have tools and parts lifted in at regular intervals if the Melevganians agree. How fast do you think you could increase production?"

"I reckon to double it within two months," said Jasken, catching on. "Those hand tools are hopelessly inefficient. Once I get the drills working, the men can concentrate on searching the debris instead of wasting time hammering at rock. Of course, that's assuming you can bring me in those parts I need. How long do you think it will take?"

"Not long. Do another check tomorrow and let me know what you want. With the Melevganians' permission I could leave the day after and return in about a week. Would you need Tambolt to help?"

"Him and a couple of the others," said Jasken, and continued as the raft drew near to the city. "I like the idea. We should celebrate it tonight. Some wine, maybe, and anything else that's going. How about the raft?"

"Forget it." Dumarest touched the engine part in his pocket. "It's useless. I'll have to ask the elect to let us use one of theirs. I can bring in a replacement when I return."

Childish banter, but to warped minds eager to hear the things they wanted it might help to ease suspicion. And it did no harm to remind the Guardians that their raft was little better than a heap of scrap metal. A lie, but one which could help to spring the trap they were in. Dumarest was uncomfortably aware of the snare which had closed around them.

Neema was aware of it too. As they entered the House of the Hanging Man she nodded to Jasken and caught Dumarest by the arm.

"Where the hell have you been? I've been waiting for you; we've all been waiting. Damn it, Earl, what kept you so long?"

"We had trouble getting away. Are you ready to leave?"

"I've been ready for over a year now, but I know what you mean." She touched the thick belt around her waist. "Yes, I'm ready."

Tambolt came toward them, his face savage. "The raft, Earl. It won't lift. The engine won't even start. I tried it and—" He broke off, looking at Dumarest's face. "Something wrong?"

"I don't know," said Dumarest coldly. "You tell me. Why did you try to start the raft?"

"I—" Tambolt swallowed. "I was testing it, that's all. Me and Haakon." He gestured toward one of the men standing in a little group beside the vehicle. "He checked and said that a part was missing. Earl! How the hell are we going to get away from here?"

Dumarest ignored him, walking over to the raft and looking inside. The interior held boxes of food, containers of water, bales and bundles together with items of clothing, vases, statues, things of price.

At his side Preleret said, softly, "I tried to stop them, Earl, but they wouldn't listen. They wouldn't have left without you, though; I'd have seen to that."

"The goods," said Dumarest. "The woman's?"

"Some. Those bales. The rest is from the house."

"Who took it? Arion? Haakon? Sekness? Tambolt?"

"Not Sekness."

Dumarest turned to face the other three. "Take these things and put them back where you found them. Tambolt, you should have known better." He thinned his lips as they made no move to obey. "You damned fools! The Hegelt know everything you do and they will talk about it. Report it, even. They have no reason to love us and can get a reward from the Melevganians for keeping watch. Try stealing and you'll wind up in the mines. If you want to know what that means, ask Jasken. He's been there."

"It's rough," said Jasken. "Do as Earl says."

"Now wait a minute!" Arion edged forward. "Tambolt said it would be all right and why shouldn't we take all that's going while we've the chance? I—"

Sekness rapped his club on the edge of the raft. It made a hard, metallic sound. "I'm with Earl," he said. "I don't like stealing, but I'm not the boss and you wouldn't have listened to me. Now the boss says it goes back. Do it!"

His club fell again, the sound menacing.

As the men began unloading the raft Dumarest said, "I

suppose you authorized this, Tambolt, before you knew you couldn't leave?"

"I just wanted to get everything ready, Earl." Tambolt tried to smile, then shrugged instead. "All right, I was wrong, but it seemed a good idea at the time. Maybe I just can't leave nice things alone, but they were sitting there just waiting to be taken. And it wasn't exactly stealing. I mean, if other traders use this house, they could have taken them. We couldn't really have been blamed. And the Melevganians have so much they wouldn't have troubled themselves about a little."

The eternal self-justification of a thief. Dumarest turned away, not bothering to argue, and found Neema again at his side.

"The raft, Earl?"

"It's working." He handed Jasken the part he had removed. "We'll be leaving in the early hours."

"Not before?"

"No. I've tried to persuade our hosts that we have no intention of leaving until the day after tomorrow. They may not believe what they heard, but we've got to keep up the pretense."

She said, shrewdly, "Is that why you made the men take back the things?"

"The fools!" His face darkened with anger. "It may be too late. If the Hegelt noticed what had happened the Melevganians could be warned by now. But if they're put back, we stand a chance. Someone might drop in for a look around. If they do, they could punish the Hegelt for lying. Or they could think it was a mistake. If the stuff isn't to be seen and is found in the raft, then we wouldn't have a hope of getting away."

"We haven't much even now," she said bleakly. "I was treating one and he talked. A manic-depressive on the slope of his cycle who wanted a boost. I gave him a little more than he bargained for. A hypnotic which I daren't use too often but carry for emergencies. They don't intend to let us go. At the moment they're playing with us, with you, that is. A cat and mouse game. Maybe you can talk them out of it, but I doubt it. The young Guardians think you killed their companions. The ones who went off with the big man."

Dumarest said, "Why would they think that?"

"The lances. You've got three of them. I saw them

and so the Hegelt must have too. You're right about them reporting to their masters. Only the Guardians carry lances and it doesn't take genius to guess where you got them from. Earl! I'm scared!"

She came into his arms and he held her, oblivious of the others, feeling the trembling of her soft body against his own. An emotional breakdown, he thought. Overstrained nerves giving way before imagined dangers. Perils all the more terrifying because, as yet, they were not real.

He said, "Can you get us some weapons, Neema? More lances, perhaps?"

"No." She stepped back, breathing deeply, her face calming as she met his eyes. "The Guardians hold them close. I had a laser when I arrived here, but it vanished. The Hegelt, I think. I could get some, I suppose, but it would be dangerous."

Too dangerous. Suspicion once aroused needed only a touch to turn into action. And, if what she had learned from her patient was true, the Guardians were watching and ready to spring. His playacting with Jasken may have lulled them. It would be greater sport to wait, to let their victims think they had an open road before snapping shut the trap. An amusement the Melevganians would appreciate. He hoped so. In their sadism lay Dumarest's only chance of escape.

From where he stood beside the raft Jasken called, "It's fixed, Earl. What happens now?"

"We wait." Dumarest studied the open area in which the raft lay. The wide doors gave to the street, stairs led upward to the living quarters. There could be traps in the floor or secret panels in the walls, but he doubted it. Such things were the product of timidity and the people of Melevgan were far from that. Insane, perhaps, but certain of their superiority. "Try to block the doors, Jasken, then stay here with Preleret on guard. Check the load and make sure we can carry everything we need to take. Dump out what's in the raft if you have to." He caught Neema's expression. "You can take what you carry, but the rest of the stuff might have to go. Do you mind?"

"No," she said. "And?"

"We're going to have a party."

It was a masquerade of shouting men and gushing wine, of food nibbled and thrown aside, of hands reaching for the soft-footed Hegelt women. Of big talk and songs and apparent drunkenness. A macabre performance for the benefit of the Hegelt and the Guardians to whom they might report. A thing promised, expected, and so provided to allay suspicion.

But not all the food was barely nibbled and cast aside. Experienced travelers knew the value of a full stomach and they had heard Dumarest's orders and knew better than the woman that nothing but a little water would remain in the raft. Life was more important than goods, and weight too precious to be wasted on baubles.

At a window Dumarest watched the sky. Night had fallen, the stars blazing in a fiery arc, and he cursed the sheets and curtains of brilliance which haloed the firmament. He wanted cloud, thick, shielding, a pall to dim the vision of any who might be watching. Later, perhaps, it might come. Later. For now they could only wait until the city quieted, until any watchers might grow drowsy at their posts.

Neema came to him. She had been a little careless with the wine as had Haakon and Arion despite the repeated warnings. Too much had been swallowed instead of being slopped and now their boisterous laughter had a genuine ring of abandon. Dumarest caught Sekness' eye and the man nodded. They would keep silent when the time came or he would take action with his club. Without weapons they were passengers; for now they could accentuate the pretense that all were getting helplessly drunk.

Neema wasn't wholly pretending. She blew out her breath and leaned against his arm as Dumarest turned from the window.

"Five years," she said. "Five lousy years. I can't believe that it's almost over. You know what I'm going to do when we reach Sargone, Earl? I'm going to have the best that money can buy. Baths, clothes, foods, wines, you name it and that's what it will be."

"You've got that already," he said.

"No. The things, maybe, but not the background. I'm sick of being served by slaves. I want people I can talk to and laugh with and know that they're doing things for me because they want to, not because they'll be whipped and maybe killed if they don't. And there are other things." She leaned a little closer. "One thing in particular. Five years in Melevgan, Earl. Can you guess what that means?"

"You told me."

"Not all of it. Not the worst part. I'm a woman Earl. I need to be loved. What's the good of money and clothes and all the rest of this junk if it doesn't fill a real need? Five years wasted, Earl. You understand?"

A woman, older than she appeared, a little drunk and more than a little sentimental. A refuge, perhaps, from imagined fears. A release from tension. Her own, private safety valve from the emotional pressures within. Dumarest remembered the environment in which she had lived, the contamination of those around her. An insidious thing which could warp without suspicion, altering viewpoints and changing logic so that the unthinkable became the commonplace, the unusual the norm.

Quietly he said, "In Sargone, Neema, you'll find all that you need."

"I've got it here, Earl. Almost. Have you ever thought about it? Everything you could ever hope for aside from one thing. And then that thing arrives and your world could be complete. And it could be, Earl, for the both of us. I can manage the Melevganians. They're insane sure, but I can manage them. And then we could really begin to live. You and me, Earl, here, in a fine house with all the servants we could use and all the things money can buy. A dream come true, Earl. Here, in the hollow of your hand. Close it and it's yours."

From terror to overconfidence, from despair to high-flying euphoria, and all in a few hours, accentuated, perhaps, by the wine. An emotional change common to manic-depressives and coupled with her betrayed paranoia. A combination which was more explosive than a bomb.

Dumarest felt his skin crawl as he looked into her eyes. They were wide, flecked with motes of shifting color, windows on a mind which drifted in unknown regions. A word and she would be at his eyes or in his arms. A rejection might cause her to turn to suicide or to run screaming in the street to condemn them all.

"A dream, Neema?" He forced himself to smile, to be casual. "But didn't you have it once?"

"I thought I had, Earl, but it didn't last. We came here knowing exactly what we had to do. For a while things were fine and then—" She shrugged. "He was weak, Earl. Stupid. He wouldn't listen to what I said. A trained fool who knew too much to take advice."

And who hung now, swinging from a gallows as a

ornament to the house in which she offered herself to another man.

"You wouldn't be weak, Earl. You're strong and know what has to be done and when to do it. A woman would be safe with you. You would take care of her, look after her, protect her. And you would do more than that, my darling. So very much more." She caught his arm. "Come with me, Earl. Come with me. Now!"

Tambolt grinned as they walked past the table, his mouth wet with wine, his eyes envious. Dumarest, conscious of the watching Hegelt, lifted a bottle and tilted it to his lips, his throat working, but swallowing nothing. He dropped the bottle with a gusting sigh, reached for another and repeated the performance, letting it fall to smash and lie in a puddle of wine.

"A song," he ordered. "Give us a song." Sound to add to the illusion of gaiety. "And how about these girls, here? Can't they dance? Music, girls, and dancing. This is a party!"

The sound rose behind him as he followed Neema from the room, dulled as he closed the door, became muted as he trod at her heels into an upstairs chamber. A couple of hours, he thought. Three at the most. He could manage her that long.

"Wine, Earl?"

The Hegelt had rearranged the room according to her instructions, given while he was at the mine. A bottle and glasses stood on a low table, the wide bed was bright with an embroidered cover, a censer stood beneath a thin spiral of rising smoke, the scent of incense hanging heavy in the air.

He took the wine, lifting it to his lips, but making no effort to swallow. Over the rim of the goblet he could see her eyes, still wide, still filled with vaguely shifting emotion.

"You love me, Earl," she said. "Say it!"

He stood, watching, silent.

"Say it!" Her voice rose a little. "I want you to love me, Earl. I love you and it isn't fair that you don't love me. You must love me. You do love me. Say it. Say, 'I love you, Neema.' Say it!"

He threw the wine into her face.

It hit, bathing her with ruby, wine running from her eyebrows, the tip of her nose and the point of her chin, dripping to the upthrust breasts beneath the low-cut gown, wet, shocking in its unexpectedness. She swayed back, blinking, hands lifting, light gleaming from the bracelets, the filigree on the backs. His left arm rose, knocking them higher as his right hand swept around to slap her sharply on the cheek.

"I told you before," he said harshly. "Use those darts on me and I'll break both of your arms."

"Earl! You—"

For a moment her sanity hung in the balance. Rage climbing, mounting, tearing at her mind with destructive fury. Rage too great to be contained. He had seen it before, in a man who had driven spikes into his blinded face and had thrown himself into a fire because of the frustration it had caused.

And then she collapsed, shuddering into his arms.

He carried her to the bed and laid her on the cover, holding her until the storm subsided, until she rose, her face wet with tears, streaked and stained by the wine.

With water he washed it clean, the golden skin now devoid of cosmetics looking haggard and a little pathetic.

"Earl!" Her hand lifted, touched her forehead. "I've got to get away from here. At times I go crazy. It's something inside, like a bursting in the mind. I can't think straight and logic has gone all to hell. I could have killed you then. I would have done it, given the chance. Nothing seemed to matter, but that. To kill you. To see you dead."

"I know," he said. "I know."

"You can't." She looked at him, her eyes clear now, a little red from her weeping. "Or perhaps you can. But you'd have reason for wanting to kill. I didn't. The Melevganians haven't, not really; they just yield to a whim. Or is it a whim?" she whispered. "Everything seems so logical and reasonable at the time. It's only afterward that it can be seen for what it is. Crazy talk and crazy behavior. And it's getting worse, Earl. I used to be able to fight against it, take drugs to control it; recently I just haven't cared."

"You'll be all right, Neema. Once we get away from here, you'll be among normal people. You could have treatment to even you out. It's nothing to worry about."

She smiled and reached out to touch his face. "You're kind, Earl. Hard, but kind. Gentle, too."

"Gentle?" His own hand touched the place where he had slapped her. The skin showed red, but there would be no bruise. "You'd better get a little rest. A few hours at least. I'll call you when it's time to go."

"No! I—" She wanted to trust him and could not call him a liar to his face. Could not put into words the doubt he knew must exist. That he would go and leave her behind. Instead she said, "My face! I must look a mess!"

Smiling, he said, "No. You look what you are. A very attractive woman."

"You think so? Earl, you really think that?" And then her arms were around him, the scent of her hair in his nostrils, the warmth of her breath against his cheek. "Don't leave me, Earl. For God's sake, don't leave me. I'm afraid. I want something to hang onto. Earl! Stay with me until it's time to go!"

CHAPTER

FIFTEEN

In the darkness the stairs were a death-trap, but if there were watchers, it was the last route they would expect him to follow. Shoulder hard against the sloping wall, Dumarest crept down the external spiral, eyes straining as he looked at the sky, the streets below. He could see no guards and the air was clear of rafts. He reached the bottom and rapped on the door. Twice, a pause, then twice more. It opened with a faint creak of timbers and in the dimness he could see the bulk of the raft, the others waiting in the vehicle, starlight catching their eyes.

Jasken had opened the door. He said, "All clear, Earl?"

"As much as it will ever be. You know what to do?"

"Lift high once we're clear and then head due west. But, Earl, Sargone lies to the south."

"We go west."

"To avoid pursuit." Jasken nodded. "A good idea. I should have thought of it."

To avoid pursuit and to head toward the Valley of Charne, but Dumarest didn't mention that. He glanced at the raft, checking that each was in his place. Jasken at the controls, Preleret with the other rifle to the left side, himself to the right. Tambolt and Sekness each with a lance at front and rear. Haakon and Arion lay in the body of the craft, breathing deeply, useless. Neema squatted beside them.

Dumarest handed her the remaining lance. "Can you use it?"

"I think so."

"Aim it like a stick. There's a button in the butt. Press it and release a missile. They've got explosive heads, so make sure they don't hit too close." He added, for the benefit of them all, "Don't start firing until I give the word. If we're stopped, I want to try bluffing our way out. Say nothing, do nothing, but keep alert. Right, Jasken, let's go!"

The engine hummed, rose to a noisy pulsing, settled

a whining drone as the raft lifted from the floor. Carefully Jasken guided it from the building, then fed more
power to the anti-gravity units. The ground fell away,
shadows passing over them from adjacent structures, drop-
ing to expose them to the burning light from the stars.
The heavens were too bright. Dumarest had hoped for
cloud, but none had come and he dared wait no longer.
Dawn must find them safely over the mountains.

Tambolt sucked in his breath.

"We're going to make it, Earl. By God, we're going to
make it!"

His words were thick, slurred a little, despite the cold
showers and drenchings he had suffered. Dumarest looked
down at the house with its grisly adornment. The Hegelt
had left an hour earlier to report, he hoped, that the party
had ended in a drunken stupor. The Guardians could have
been deluded. If so, their only real danger lay in running
into a random patrol.

They rose still higher, the city falling beneath until it
looked a garish toy, lights showing the shape of buildings,
the tiny figures of Hegelt at their never-ending task of
keeping the place clean. Dumarest leaned over the side, his
eyes narrowed.

"Neema!"

She joined him immediately, her hair brushing his cheek.
"What is it, Earl?"

"That crowd down there. Normal?"

"Nothing's normal in Melevgan. It could be the start
of a hunt—sometimes one of them is crazy enough to
volunteer for quarry, or sometimes, for no apparent reason, they gang up on one of their own kind. Usually someone they reckon may have lived too long. Or it could be a
group-session. They gather, start keening, and whip themselves into a frenzy." She drew in her breath, an inward
sigh of annoyance. "I can't be sure. It's too far away. It
worries you, Earl?"

At a time like this everything was a cause for worry.
They had lifted high when leaving the city to escape
observation; a raft heading upward was invisible to anyone
not looking at the sky. But other rafts, lower, might
spot them occluding the stars as they headed west. To
drop lower might be safer, but they would lose maneuver-
ability close to the ground. And, if seen, could arouse suspicion.

All they could do was to remain alert and trust to luc[k]
It ran out halfway to the mountains.

Preleret saw it first. He said, "Something coming, Ea[rl]
From the left and below."

A dark shape touched with starlight. A large raft fille[d]
with armored men.

Tambolt said, "We could blast it, Earl. Spray it wit[h]
missiles from the lances. Hit them before they know it[.]"

"No."

"But—"

"Shut up! Don't talk and keep those weapons out o[f]
sight."

Two rifles with fifteen-shot capacity. Three lance[s]
with ten missiles each. Thirty shots aimed by inexperience[d]
hands. Two-thirds of them would never reach the targe[t]
The rest might kill, maim, and, perhaps, smash the engine[.]
Then would come the return fire from those who ha[d]
managed to survive. The alarm would have been given an[d]
they would be defenseless before another attack.

And, as yet, the raft hadn't seen them. It was ridin[g]
level and several hundred feet below. With luck it woul[d]
pass.

In the body of the raft Haakon turned, rose on al[l]
fours and shouted, "Wine! Bring more wine! I want mor[e]
wine!"

Sekness moved, his club lifting to fall with a dul[l]
crack, but the damage had been done. An armored hea[d]
tilted, starlight showing the slits, the dark patches beneat[h]
which were eyes. A gloved hand raised, pointing; a lanc[e]
aimed itself; another, a dozen.

Dumarest said quickly, "Sing. Tambolt, Jasken, preten[d]
you're drunk. The rest of you drop—and hide thos[e]
weapons."

He lowered his own rifle as the raft below swung u[p]
to ride level, leaning over the edge, grinning, waving hi[s]
hand in cheerful greeting.

"Hi, there! A nice night for a ride. You should have
been at the party. We had quite a time. Wine, women,
song." He jerked his hand to where the others stood,
bawling. "Want to join in?"

"You will halt immediately!"

"Sure." Dumarest waved at Jasken. "You heard the man.
He wants to join us. He can't do it while we keep moving."

"And be silent."

"The singing? Anything you say, my lord. We're going to work for you, did you know that? Me, these two, the others we left behind in the house." He shook his head, appearing to regain control of himself. "My lords! If we have offended, we apologize. Have I the honor of talking to Tars Boras?"

"You know him?"

"I have had the honor of his company. It was he who gave us permission to test our raft tonight. He was most gracious."

For a moment the armored figure standing upright in the raft stared blankly at Dumarest, the closed visor giving him the appearance of a bizarre robot. Then he said, "You will turn and follow me back to the city. If you deviate from our flight path, you will immediately be destroyed."

"As you command, my lord," said Dumarest. "As you wish, so shall it be."

Jasken said, "Earl?"

"Do as he says, but as you turn win us a little height."

Dumarest crouched as the raft swung in a tight circle, moving across the interior to touch Preleret on the shoulder. He kept his voice low.

"They've got us covered. If we start anything and don't get them first, they'll blast us all to hell. Sekness, how are you with a rifle?"

"I can use one."

"Take mine. It's ready to shoot. Semiautomatic—just aim and pull the trigger. Move over to the right. Preleret, you take the left. Rise when I gave the word and take care of anyone aiming anything at us. I'll see to their raft." Dumarest picked up the lance Sekness had discarded.

Neema said, "Can I help?"

"No. You stay out of this. Tambolt, you cover Jasken. If anyone tries to get him, you get them first. But don't use the lance unless you have to. Ready?" He peered over the edge of the raft. "Now!"

He rose, the lance in his hands, the point steadying as he aimed the shaft. Ahead armored figures held leveled lances, but he gambled that they would be slow to open fire. Slow enough for the two marksmen to take care of them with the rifles. He heard the sharp explosions, saw the Melevganians fall backward as bullets tore through their decorative armor, others turning to fall under the merciless fire.

As they fell, he was touching the button beneath his thumb, missiles spouting from the tip of the lance. Four shots, all concentrated on the driver and the controls of the vehicle. As they exploded, he yelled to Jasken.

"Turn! Lift! Take evasive action!"

Missiles streaked toward them as the man obeyed, lines of fire cutting the air beneath and to one side. One struck the rear edge of the raft, flame gushing over the side as it exploded against the bottom. Tambolt shouted, lifted his lance, swore as Dumarest tore it from his hands.

"What the hell are you doing?"

"Saving our fire-power." Dumarest looked back at the other raft. It was tilted, slowly falling, men clinging to the sides. His missiles had wrecked the controls. "We've had our share of luck. The next time they come, we'll need every bullet and missile we have."

"If they come."

"They'll come," said Dumarest grimly. "Keep watch while I check the damage."

The stray missile had hit a few feet from the extreme rear of the raft, the explosives tearing a jagged patch. Arion's head had been lying where it had hit. The raft rose a little as Dumarest threw his body over the side.

"Can't you get us higher, Jasken?"

"I'm trying. That missile didn't do us any good. We've lost some lift."

"Do the best you can." Dumarest stooped over Haakon. His legs were singed, but otherwise he seemed unhurt aside from the lump on his head where Sekness had clubbed him. He groaned as Dumarest slapped his cheeks.

"What—"

"Up! Hang over the side. Be sick if you want to, but get active. Up, damn you! Up!"

"My head!" The man struggled upright, his eyes bloodshot, creased with pain. "Where's Arion?"

"Dead and over the side. You were lucky. Try to stay that way." Dumarest looked at the woman. "Give him some water, drugs too if you have any. I want every eye we've got open and on the lookout. When the Melevganians come, I want to see them before they see us."

They arrived as the raft neared the summit of the mountains, a black oblong against the stars, flying high and fast and intent on the kill. Plumed helmets showed

over the sides and the starlight glinted from the points of
bristling lances.

Tambolt said, "We could drop, Earl. Get below the
mountains and use them as a shield."

"No."

"It would give us a chance." His voice was firm, his
semidrunkenness evaporated by tension. "We might even
be able to land."

A possibility Dumarest had considered and rejected.
They could land and hide and wait out the day and hope
that they wouldn't be spotted. But to land in starlight on
the side of a jagged mountain without lights to guide them
and no assurance they would find a suitable place was to
tempt luck too far.

"No," he said again. "And we can't drop. If we do
and they spot us, we'll be pinned against the wall of the
mountain."

"Then all we can do is to hope they don't see us,"
said Tambolt. "Hope—and pray." He stared upward, his
hands clenched as the other raft drew near and passed
overhead. "They've missed us. Earl, they—" He broke
off, cursing as light blazed around them. "What the hell's
that?"

A flare, dropped from the other raft, drifting down on
its parachute and bathing them in the eye-bright glow
of burning magnesium.

They had seconds before the heavens would rain
fire.

"Move!" Dumarest yelled at Jasken as he snatched the
rifle from Sekness' hands. "Preleret, get that light!"

He dropped to one knee, aiming at the raft and the
helmeted heads behind the bristling lances, squinting
against the glare which dazed his vision. The rifle kicked
against his shoulder as he sent a stream of bullets to smash
into slotted visors. Missiles flared up beside him as Tambolt joined in, trying to destroy the armored men before
they could open fire.

Preleret grunted, aimed, fired, and fired again. The
flare exploded into a shower of burning fragments which
fell, dying, to the ground below.

"Quick, Jasken! Get under them!" Dumarest threw
aside the empty rifle and snatched up a lance. Haakon
rose, wavering.

"A gun," he said. "Give me a gun."

His head dissolved. His chest puffed out in a mess of blood, ribs and internal organs, spattering fragments and scraps of lung as the missile exploded. Others followed, a rain of streaking fire which passed to one side as Jasken turned the raft. Sekness cried out, looked at the ripped hole in his side, and then, without a sound, toppled over the edge. A missile, lucky or more carefully aimed, had exploded against the rear where he had stood.

Two more flares illuminated the night. Dumarest ignored them, concentrating on his aim. Fire blossomed against the base of the raft above, ripping metal just behind where he estimated the controls to be. More gushed a little to one side, then he held down the stud and emptied the weapon, sending the missiles through the widened hole.

Two passed right through; the others met opposition. He heard screams, the roar of explosions, and the sound of grating metal. A Melevganian toppled over the edge, wailing as he fell. Another leaned over, grotesquely misshapen, showering a sticky rain. The raft lurched to one side, fell a little, veered sluggishly as it turned.

"Under them!" snapped Dumarest. "Stay under them!"

Their altitude was to his advantage—as long as it was not too great. They could not fire without leaning over the edge and exposing themselves and, if their target was too close, couldn't bring their lances to bear. But there was a danger and he recognized it.

"Preleret! Watch that hole I made. If anyone tries to use it, get them."

"I'm low on shots, Earl."

"Then make them all count. Use a lance if you have to." He threw aside the one he had used. There were two others: the one Tambolt had used probably almost empty, the other full. Ten missiles. It should be more than enough.

Jasken said, "Earl!"

The other raft had twisted again, jerking sidewise and rising a little so that it was a little to one side. Abruptly it fell.

Dumarest fired as he saw the raised lances, aiming not at the helmets, but at the side of the raft below them. The missiles would explode on impact, and the armor they wore would protect the Guardians from flying fragments, but the concussion would daze and, perhaps, stun.

The lance was inaccurate and he had no missiles to waste on elusive targets.

The thing was to stun, confuse, to kill if he could, but, above all, to prevent an accurate return fire. A rain of missiles which would reach the raft and blast its occupants into smoking shreds.

Speed alone was the only real defense. Six lances were leveled toward him, their tips circling a little as the Melevganians aimed the shafts. Dumarest fired at once, sending as many missiles to roar in a continuous explosion against the side of the raft, hearing the crack of Preleret's rifle, Tambolt's hysterical shout.

"Dodge, man! For God's sake, get out of the way!"

Dumarest felt the raft drop beneath him as Jasken cut the lift. It fell as an armored figure rose, his lance streaming flame. A streak of fire cut past Dumarest's head; another ended in a gout of flame at his rear. Two more reached for Jasken, a third slamming into the metal at his side.

Then the armored shape dissolved into bursting metal and flesh as Dumarest fired. He had three missiles left. He sent them all into the raft at where he guessed the engine to be. The explosions grew, turned into flame, licking, roaring high as the raft spun away hopelessly out of control . . . to tilt and shower bizarre figures from the interior, screaming as they fell to spatter on the rocks below.

"Earl!" Jasken was dying, his voice a raw thread of agony. He crouched against the side of the raft, a pool of blood around his feet from the gaping wounds left by the fragments which had ripped open his stomach. "The controls, Earl. I can't handle the controls!"

"Take them," said Dumarest to Tambolt. "Neema?"

She had been hurt, blood on her shoulder, the front of her dress, her left arm hanging limply at her side. She knelt, examining the engineer, rising with a helpless shake of her head.

"I can't help him, Earl. A missile got my bag. Me too. We have no drugs, nothing to ease his pain. He's suffering. My God, he's suffering, but there's nothing we can give him."

Nothing but the pressure of a hand, the fingers hard against the carotids to bring swift unconsciousness and merciful oblivion. Dumarest eased the man to the floor of the raft, laying him down where Haakon lay in an untidy heap.

"We'll bury them in soft ground somewhere," he said. "Somewhere under a tree with a stone as a marker."

Tambolt said, "On the way to Sargone?"

"On the way to the Valley of Charne," said Dumarest flatly. "I've still got to find Jondelle."

CHAPTER

SIXTEEN

Konba Tach rose as usual a little before dawn, ate the food his wife had prepared, and then went out to his farm which clung to the side of the mountain. It was, he felt, going to be a good day. Already the mist which filled the valley with the setting of each sun was thinning, lowering to show other farms to the sides and below . . . a collection of small patches of ground, painstakingly leveled, walled, and planted with neatly arranged crops. Unga beans, mostly, with some klwem, artash, and a few shrubs of prenchet which provided a useful narcotic. There were herbs also and bushes which bore leaves for the making of tisanes, tall grasses which could be beaten and dyed and woven into delicate fabrics. And flowers. Everywhere, in the valley, there were flowers.

He stooped over a swollen bloom and inhaled the sweet perfume. Rising, he looked at the raft which had arrived with the sun.

It was not a local vehicle. The sides were scarred, torn, the metal showing the marks of violence. Those within looked in little better shape . . . a woman, pale, her left arm bandaged and in a sling . . . the man beside her, tall in his gray clothing, his eyes watchful . . . two others who drooped as if from exhaustion. Travelers from a far place, Konba Tach guessed. Strangers to the valley. Perhaps they had been caught in the storms common to the Wendelt Plain; but no matter who they were or why they looked as they did, custom demanded they be offered food and refreshment, the hospitality of his home.

Bowing, he said, "Strangers, you are welcome."

"Is this the Valley of Charne?"

"It is. My name is Konba Tach. My wife and children are not yet at work, but greet you in my name. If you will alight, it will give me honor to attend to your needs."

"You are more than kind," said Dumarest. The neatly arranged plants betrayed the poverty which must exist here, forcing the use of every inch of ground. "We gladly accept your offer of refreshment. Have you hot water? Bandages?" He gestured to where Neema stood. "The woman has been hurt."

"All shall be provided." Konba Tach lifted his voice as he gave orders to the woman peering from the open door of the house set into the flank of the mountain. "Now, if you will follow me?"

They washed in a tub half-filled with water which stung like ice, the bath both refreshing and stimulating appetites. The food was hot, consisting of beans flavored with herbs and mixed with succulent fragments of pulpy vegetable. It filled but did not satisfy, a low-protein diet which gave little energy and was mental poison to a growing intelligence. The reason, perhaps, why Konba Tach remained on the farm, why his son would follow him, his daughters continuing the same life. A family trapped in the ways of their forebears, struggling constantly to exist on a patch of ground leveled from the side of a mountain instead of striking out to the more fertile plains beyond.

And yet they seemed happy enough, the house clean, the children neat, the woman deft as she cleared the table and provided cups of fragrant tisane.

"That was good," said Tambolt. "The first hot meal we've had in how long, Earl? Ten days?"

"Twelve," said Preleret. His hands shook a little as he lifted his cup. "Ten days since we buried the others."

A long time to travel without supplies. They had drunk when they had found water, eaten a few roots and juiceless berries, remaining constantly on the alert for questing Melevganian rafts.

Tambolt refilled his cup from the pot of tisane.

"Well, we made it. We're safe now. We can get the raft fixed or buy another one and head to Sargone. Right, Preleret?"

"When Earl says."

"The boy." Tambolt frowned. "The Valley of Charne is three hundred miles long. There is one major and two minor cities and God knows how many farms and settlements. How the hell are you going to find one small boy in a place like this?"

"If he's here, I'll find him," said Dumarest. To Neema he said, "Let's take a look at that arm."

It was bad. Beneath the crusted bandages the flesh was rn, imbedded with minute fragments from the bursting issile, the tissue tender and inflamed. Dumarest lowered is head, sniffing, catching the sickly odor of putrefaction. e reached for water and bandages, his face impassive.

"It's bad," said Tambolt. "If she isn't careful, she uld lose the arm, her life as well. At the hospital in argone she could have the best of attention."

"She'll get it," said Preleret. "They must have doctors in e Valley."

"Sure, but—" Tambolt broke off, his eyes thoughtful. s Dumarest finished the bandaging he said, "Earl? Could have a word with you? In private?"

Outside he walked to where the raft stood in a patch f crushed grass. The mist was lower now, showing the oor of the valley, vapor pluming to hide the shapes of uildings which stood like toys dwarfed by the immensity f the mountains.

He looked at them for a moment, then said, "Earl, ust where does Preleret stand? As regards our deal, I ean."

"Deal?"

"The money you hope to get for the boy. I know why ou're after him and I'm with you all the way. We've done ell, but we could double it easily. Maybe more. That id must be worth a fortune to whoever wants him. Once e find the goods we—"

"Jondelle isn't 'goods,'" said Dumarest harshly. "He's boy. He isn't something to be found and offered to the ighest bidder. He was stolen, his mother shot, his step-ather killed. He isn't a bag of jewels or a bundle of loot. e is a human being. Remember that."

"Sure," said Tambolt hastily. "It was just a manner f speaking. I feel for the kid as much as you do. But here does Preleret fit in?"

"He's willing to help."

"For free?" Tambolt shrugged. "Well, I'll leave it up o you, Earl. Maybe we could give him something for is trouble. A share, a tenth, say; I'll go to that. But if e gets greedy, we'll have to cut him down. You agree?"

Dumarest looked down at his hand. He was gripping e side of the raft and the knuckles were white. He re-oved it, walking to the wall, looking at the slabs of

stone, the tiny lichens growing in the windblown d
accumulated between the cracks.

He said, "First we have to find the boy. What v
do with what I get for him can wait, but I promise y
this. Half of what I get for him is yours. I'll take care
Preleret."

"Fair enough, Earl. And the rest? What we got for t
goods?"

"After expenses we cut it three ways."

"Three?" Tambolt frowned. "That seems high, Ea
Too high for a man straight out of Lowtown. Why n
give him the High passage you promised?"

"He gets a third," snapped Dumarest. "After expense
If it hadn't been for him, Tambolt, we'd be dead no
His rifle gave us the edge when we needed it most. A thi
and I'm not going to argue about it."

Tambolt shrugged. "All right, Earl. You're the boss."

"Yes," said Dumarest. "Remember that."

Preleret was asleep when they returned to the house. H
lay spread across the table, his head cradled in his arm
his breathing stentorian. He woke, blinking as Dumare
touched his shoulder.

"Earl?"

"Go and dip your head in the tub outside. We're leavin
You can sleep later in a soft bed with clean sheets
Dumarest turned to Neema. "How do you feel?"

"Dopey." She held a saffron pod in her hand ar
chewed on another. "Our hostess gave me something
ease the pain. It does, too, but I'm feeling all detached
if I'm floating."

"Prenchet," explained Konba Tach. "It can be a gre
comfort in times of distress." His eyes widened as I
looked at the gem Dumarest dropped into his palm. "M
lord?"

"A gift. For you, your wife, your children." Dumare
knew better than to pay for the hospitality they had re
ceived. Poor as he was their host had his pride. "Clothe
tools, and seeds. Money to take you to a new farm," I
hinted. "Fertile ground and animals to supply meat f
your table. If you accept it, I shall gain honor."

Konba Tach bowed, hiding the glow in his eyes.

"Sell it to an honest man," said Dumarest. "Bett
still, deposit it as collateral in a bank. . . . Where is
tavern known as the Sumba?"

"I do not know, my lord." Konba Tach was apologetic.
"Rarely do I leave the farm and we have no money for the
things to be found in taverns."

"A doctor, then?"

"Gar Cheng is a good man. Descend to the floor of
the valley, head to the west; he lives at the house with a
triple pagoda. On foot the journey takes a day. With a
raft less than an hour." He bowed again. "My lord, may
good fortune attend each step you take."

"And may happiness fill your days."

Gar Cheng was a small, wizened, snapping turtle of a
man with a straggle of thinning hair and a mouth which
looked as if it had tasted a rotten fruit. He hissed as he
examined Neema's arm, his dark eyes accusing as he stared
at Dumarest.

"This woman should have received immediate medical
attention. To have neglected the injury was inexcusable.
Why have you waited so long?"

"We had no choice, Doc." The narcotic she had chewed
had slurred the woman's voice. "And we had no drugs
or prophylactics. Don't blame Earl, blame circumstance."
She began to giggle.

"Prenchet," said Dumarest. "She'd chewed a pod before
I could stop her." He held out the other. "Bad?"

"Undesirable. In its raw state prenchet is a strongly
addictive narcotic. At times I wonder how the hill farmers
manage to resist its lure." The doctor shrugged. "Well, no
matter. The damage has been done and, at least, she will
have interesting dreams." He probed at the mangled flesh.
"Have you money?"

"Yes."

"That is well. If you hadn't, I would still treat the
woman, but in that case all I could do would be to ampu-
tate. Later you could buy a prosthetic or a regraft, but that,
of course, would be up to you. As it is, I can perform
extensive surgery which, coupled with the use of hormones
and slow-time, will repair the damage. Such treatment is
expensive. Aside from the use of my skill there are others
to pay and the things I need do not come cheap."

"Get them," said Dumarest. "Do whatever is needed.
She can pay."

"In advance?" Gar Cheng frowned at the gems Dumarest

placed in his hand. "I'm not a jeweler. These stones me
nothing to me. Have you no cash?"

Neema giggled again. "What's he want, Earl? Money
She tugged at the belt around her waist. It revealed t
flash of jewels, the glint of metal. "Here's money. Ho
much do you want? Five hundred stergals? A thousan
Help yourself."

Dumarest helped himself to a handful of coins. "Tw
hundred," he said, counting. "I need it. All right, Neema

"Sure." She swayed, eyes closing. "Anything you war
Earl. Anything you want. Me, the loot, anything. Ju
ask and it's yours."

Gar Cheng took the belt from her hands. She was la
breathing deeply, already lost in narcotic dreams. "I w
take care of this. Later, when she has recovered, she ca
settle my bill. And now, if you will excuse me, there
much to do and no more time should be wasted."

Outside the others waited in the raft. Preleret w
asleep; Tambolt nodded as he sat at the controls. Reactic
had caught them, the effect of the food, the relief of ha
ing arrived safe at the Valley of Charne. Dumarest fe
the grit in his eyes, the sapping ache of strength used an
almost exhausted. He wanted to find the tavern, the b
man, the boy, but caution dictated delay.

The big man had killed and could kill again. He woul
be fresh and alert and perhaps suspicious of stranger
Against him an exhausted man would stand little chanc
and a dead man was useless to Jondelle.

Tambolt said, "What now, Earl?"

"Sleep," said Dumarest, deciding. "A few hours
least."

"And then?"

"We find the Sumba."

CHAPTER

SEVENTEEN

It was not what he had expected. The Charnian in the
mine had called it a tavern, but it was far more than that.
A vastly sprawling place of bars, and baths, and discrete
rooms . . . of open spaces and amusements, fountains and
tinkling lanterns. In the mist it looked ghostly, unreal,
patches of light swelling to vanish in blurs of fading
color, others blooming to take their place. By day it was
an intricate complex of rooms and halls and covered ways,
by night a fairylike palace of music, perfume, and myste-
rious enigma.

"One man," said Tambolt. "In a place like this."

"We'll find him," said Dumarest. "If he's here. You're
good at that kind of thing, Tambolt. And you've got eyes
and ears, Preleret. Move around, watch, ask a few questions. You're looking for a big man, almost a giant. Heeg
Euluch. If you spot him, don't talk to him and try not
to arouse suspicion."

Preleret said, "And if we find him?"

"There's a bar, the Paradisa Room. If I'm not there,
wait for me. I'll drop in as often as I can. Move now.
We've wasted enough time."

Too much, thought Dumarest as they moved away,
vanishing almost at once in the swirling mist. A whole
day . . . and yet it couldn't be helped. They had needed
the rest and a place like the Sumba wouldn't come really
alive until the night. If Euluch followed the usual pattern
of his kind, now was the best time to find him.

He stepped ahead, cautiously, hearing water gurgle to
his right, a gusting sigh from his left. Fountains and
wind-operated bubble-throwers, both devoid of their visual
magic in the clinging mist which filled the valley. The
path grated underfoot, the sound changing from the rasp
of gravel to the crunch of shell, to the ting of metal, to
the splash of rain. An attendant, his eyes masked by fog-

penetrating goggles, loomed from one side. He carried club.

"You are bemused, sir?"

"A little."

"Then you are new to the Sumba. The paths tell discerning ear which direction they take. Music towar the palace of joy, light, enchanting, a little more somb on the return. To the gaming rooms? Then we have th unmistakable clink of coin, the familiar rattle of dice. T the baths? What else but the tinkle of water. To the bar The gush of wine and the susurration of murmuring voice A most cunning introduction, as I think you will agree. B then, the Sumba is no ordinary place."

"No," said Dumarest.

"Of course for those who do not care to wander th night the inner complex yields on to each and every roo and chamber of intriguing delight. If I may guide you, si I will show you the way."

"I'd like to look around," said Dumarest. "Is th possible?"

"At any time during the day, most certainly. At night' The figure shrugged. "The mist holds a magic which mu not be dissipated. A pleasant companion gains an adde mystery when wreathed with the vapors of Charne. T stroll along the paths is an adventure for foot and e with each step filled with potential romance. There ar ladies here, sir, of high quality who would not care to b exposed to eyes which stare too hard and look too lon; Discretion, sir, is all, and in the Sumba we are mo discreet. Wander as you will, but wander as you are. Th rule, sir, and rules must not be broken. Those locked i the passion of love must rest assured that none can se better than they. And love, sir, on soft couches all aroun which only a questing foot can find, is easy to find fo one who stands and waits."

Harpies haunting the mist eager to sell fleshy delight and perhaps more than harpies. Or, no, the guards woul take care of that with their goggles and clubs. Here th rich and depraved would be safe from those eager to ro without finesse.

"A large place," said Dumarest. He had been taken fo a stranger seeking casual amusement. A ready-made ex cuse and a natural protection.

"Very large," agreed the guard. "If you wish, I coul

ind you pleasant company. A girl from Ikinold, perhaps?"

"Or a boy from Relad?"

For a moment the man hesitated, then said, regretfully, 'A boy, sir, yes, but not from Relad. Shall I—"

"Later," said Dumarest quickly. "First I shall look nside. If you will guide me?"

Triple doors kept out the mist, polarized so as to :eep in the light. Inside it was warm and dry with only a iint of vapor marring the clarity of the air. The Paradisa Room was a transposed portion of jungle with false vegetation covering walls and ceiling, a dozen varieties of ruit hanging low, mechanical simulacra moving, peering rom behind leaves and boles to vanish as soon as seen. The iir was heavy with tropical odors, stirring with the sub-iudible beat of drums, of rain, of distant thunder.

The bar was in the shape of split trees, the drinks served n plastic fashioned into the likeness of fruit shells. Duma-est ordered and sat nursing his drink. He did not have o wait long. A girl, wearing only a string of beads and i dress of synthetic skin which left one shoulder and >reast bare, sat beside him. The dress was cut to the hip ind showed the silken sheen of her thigh. Her feet were •ainted blue, the nails red, the soles a dusty green. The notif was continued over her body and gave her face a nask-like appearance.

"You are alone," she said. "In the Sumba no one hould be alone. For a stergal I will talk to you for hirty minutes. For ten I am yours for an hour to do with s you please."

"I am looking for a friend of mine," said Dumarest. 'Perhaps you know him. A big man. Heeg Euluch."

"You may call me Odenda. For a stergal I will talk o you for thirty minutes."

"Go to hell," said Dumarest. He caught the bartender's ye and waved him over. The man stared blankly as he epeated his question.

"Euluch? Never heard of him. You want another drink?"

Dumarest dropped a coin on the bar. "No drink. Just nswers. If you know the big man, tell him a friend vants to see him. I'll be moving around."

He had told the others to be cautious, but he made no ittempt at caution himself. He passed through the rooms, uying unwanted drinks, asking always the same question, lways receiving the same answer. No one knew the big

man. No one knew anyone named Heeg Euluch. But some
one would carry the word and, maybe, the man would be
curious enough to show himself.

If he was here. If the man in the mine had told
the truth. If he just wasn't wasting his time.

Back in the Paradisa Room Preleret was waiting. He
caught Dumarest's eye, saw the faint signal, and shook his
head. Tambolt came in a moment later. He grinned at
Odenda, then looked at Dumarest with amazement.

"Earl! What the hell are you doing here? I thought you
were busy with—well, you know. How did you make
out?"

"Fine. I was lucky, Famur wasn't. The big one and
Urlat got away. You want a drink?"

Tambolt had a drink. Odenda came to Dumarest and
slipped her arm through his. Softly she said, "One stergal
and we talk. Ten and you play, if that is your desire.
Twenty and I will tell you what you want to know."

"I told you once—"

"—to go to hell. Yes, I heard you. Are we in business
mister, or not?" In the painted face the eyes were
hard, the lips parted to show teeth too white and too
sharp. In the dim light of the bar she reminded Dumarest
of a Melevganian.

He said, "Twenty stergals for an introduction to a
man I want to do business with? You must be crazy."

"Ten then."

"Five—payable after we've met."

"Mister, when that happens I won't be around. Give
me the money." She tucked it somewhere within her
dress. "Heeg Euluch is a big man in more ways than one.
He owns part of the Sumba. Are you really his friend?"

"Money is. I can help him to get it."

"If you can't, then start running." She shrugged and
Dumarest made no effort to move. "Well, it's your neck.
Go to the gaming room. Play a little spectrum. Wait."

The game was a seven-card deal, two draws, the object
being to make a complete spectrum, red low, violet high.
A game with too many variables for Dumarest's liking, but
he played as ordered. After thirty minutes in which he
won a hundred stergals a voice whispered in his ear.

"All right, mister. You want to meet Heeg Euluch?
Come with us."

Two of them, young, lithe with the arrogance of those accustomed to power. They led him from the gaming room down long passages, through doors, and into an empty chamber. Another door and he faced a man behind a desk. A big man with hair tight against his skull. Eyes almost lost in folds of fat, the material of his shirt tight across his shoulders.

As the men who had escorted Dumarest left the room he said, "You wanted to see me? I'm Heeg Euluch."

Dumarest frowned. The voice was too high, even allowing for the distortion of a helmet. And there was a softness about the shoulders, a weakness about the chin.

He said, "Stand up."

"What? Now—"

"Up," snapped Dumarest. "Get on your feet!"

The man grunted, rising to stand behind the desk. He was big, his paunch round, sagging, thighs like the boles of trees.

"All right," said Dumarest. "It's polite to stand when greeting a visitor. Now let's end this charade. You're not Heeg. Where is he?"

The man shrugged. "Don't take it hard. We had to be sure you knew him. Heeg! Come out now!"

A door at the rear opened and a giant stepped into the room.

He was huge with muscle where the other was bloated with fat. His head towered, the features hard, his mouth a slash of savagery against the thrust of his jaw. A man who would think nothing of killing, cheating, abandoning those who worked with him, of stealing a child—if by doing so, he could gain personal advantage.

"I'm Heeg." His voice was deep, resonant. "You seem to know me, but I don't know you. Who told you where to find me?"

"Sheem. He wasn't happy at the way you left him."

"That's his grief. And?"

"I was wondering what happened to Chen Urlat. We had a deal going."

"Forget it. Urlat's dead."

Urlat and the two others who had been in the raft. The Melevganians who had probably been lasered down together with Urlat and dumped over the side so as to leave the big man in undisputed possession of Jondelle.

Dumarest said, "I've come to buy something—you know what. Are you able to sell?"

"Maybe." The hard eyes grew thoughtful. To the fat man Heeg said, "You've got something to do. Do it."

"But, Heeg—"

"Go and get us some wine. Move!"

"Good," said Dumarest as the man left. "We don't need witnesses. You have the boy?"

"And if I have?"

"I'll buy him. Ten thousand stergals. The cash in your hand by noon tomorrow. A deal?"

"There's a door behind you," said Heeg. "Get on the other side of it."

"All right," said Dumarest. "I was keeping it low. You can't blame me for that. Deliver the boy and I'll put twenty thousand in your hand."

He had hit the right level. The man frowned, greed bright in his eyes, then he shook his head.

"I want thirty."

A bargaining price and inwardly Dumarest relaxed. The man could be lying, the boy could have been passed on if that had been the original intention, but he doubted it. A man like Heeg would hold to out the last, upping the price as high as the traffic would bear. Or he could be trying a bluff; the boy could be dead. He felt the tension return at the thought of it. With an effort he remained calm.

"You ask too much. The market won't stand it and I've got to get my profit. Of course, if you want to pass him on and get robbed on the deal, that's your business. How much were you offered? Ten? Twelve?" He caught the betraying tension, the tiny, revealing signs learned from endless hours facing others across countless gambling tables. "I'm offering a fat profit and no risk. Just hand over the boy and I'll take care of the other end." He paused and added, casually, "Do I know who arranged this?"

"You're smart," grated Heeg. "Maybe too damned smart. Make it twenty-five."

"Twenty." It would be a mistake to agree too quickly.

"I can get that with no grief. It's just a matter of waiting. And why should I deal with you anyway? I don't know you. Why should I take your word?".

"About what?" Dumarest shrugged. "The money? You don't hand over the boy until you get it. You don't know me? What the hell does that matter? I know you and what you did. You jumped the gun, is all. You beat me to it. Well, it happens. You spend time arranging a deal and then someone gets in first. But you're being sold short. So why not cut out the middle man? I'm willing to buy what you hold. Twenty thousand. A deal?"

Heeg scowled. A big man who relied on brute strength rather than mental agility, a greedy man and therefore weak.

"Add five and the boy's yours. It's my last word. Take it or leave it."

"I'll take it, but I've got to see him." Dumarest met the other man's eyes. "I want to know he's still alive," he said coldly. "Dead he's useless to you and me both. I don't intend buying something I can't sell. Where is he?"

"Here," said the big man. "In the Sumba. In the Mirage."

CHAPTER
EIGHTEEN

He looked very small and very pathetic as he sat in a small room containing only a bed, a rug, a single chair. He wore a jumper suit of dull green, pointed shoes on his feet, the beads around his neck the only touch of cheerful color. Instinctively Dumarest took a step toward him, grunting as he collided with a smooth, unyielding surface.

Heeg laughed. "Neat, isn't it? You see the kid, but he can't see you. You can watch him, but you can't touch him or talk to him. Well, there he is. Twenty-five thousand and he's yours. Satisfied?"

"No." Dumarest reached out and touched the surface depicting the boy. A mirror, he guessed, portraying a scene relayed by other mirrors and lenses. He looked upward and saw a disk of light. "This could be a projection. The boy could be dead and this a taped recording."

"It isn't."

"I've got to be sure. I want to touch the boy, talk to him."

"You want too damn much," snapped Heeg. "You've seen the mechandise. You can talk to him when I see the money. Have it here at noon tomorrow and we'll make the swap. Now get the hell out of here. That door will take you outside."

The mist was thick, clammy now that the night was old and the air chill. Dumarest heard the path beneath his boots, the thin shattering of crystal, too reminiscent of a child's tears. Had Jondelle cried? Sitting like an animal in his cage of a room, had he known the bleakness of despair? Or was he numbed by events beyond his experience, withdrawing into his own world of private fantasy, finding comfort in the familiar touch of a bedcover, the beads placed by his mother around his neck.

A guard loomed from the darkness. "Sir?"

"The Paradisa Room. Direct me."

It was busier now, men and women filling the air with

strained gaiety. Preleret nursed a drink in a corner. He caught Dumarest's eye, finished his drink, and went outside. Five minutes later Dumarest followed.

In the mist he said, "Get Tambolt. The boy's here. I've seen him. I'm going to get him out."

From a locked building, probably guarded, in an area shielded by mist. But Heeg would not have trusted too many with his secret. And he could be overconfident, planning, no doubt, to take the money and keep the boy.

Waiting for the others to return Dumarest prowled the area. From somewhere a woman laughed, the sound sensual in the mist. There was a creak and the echo of hard breathing. Running feet filled the air with a medley of sounds and a mechanism nearby filled the mist with a gush of cloying perfume.

He halted, looking helpless, swearing as he turned, apparently hopelessly lost.

"Is anyone here? I need help."

A shadow thickened, revealed itself as a guard. "Sir, I am at your ser—"

The smooth voice broke as Dumarest slammed his fist into the stomach. As the man doubled he struck again, the edge of his stiffened hand impacting the nerves in the side of the neck. The man was not dead, but would remain unconscious for an hour. Dumarest tore off the goggles, donned them, rose gripping the club. Around him the grounds of the Sumba sprang to life.

It was a pale, eerily green scene, people showing as warm figures against the trees, the buildings. Other guards stood or strolled at the side of the echoing paths. Dumarest followed one, lifting an arm in casual greeting as the man turned. Goggled, dressed in neutral gray, the club at his side, he looked enough like a companion to lull the man's suspicions. By the time the guard realized his mistake it was too late. Then another, and Dumarest walked with spare goggles and clubs to where Preleret and Tambolt stood blinking in the mist.

"Take these." He handed over the equipment. "Stay off the paths and follow me. If anyone tries to stop us, get them before they can give the alarm."

The building where he had seen the boy lay a short distance from the main complex, joined to it by a covered passage. It was a low place with a roof almost flat, a hexagonal structure with blank walls and two doors.

Dumarest passed the one by which he had left and halted at the other. It was on the far side, away from the main buildings, faced by a pool of water set in a sloping lawn. Beyond it rose the high wall of the enclosure.

From the other side of the building came the sound of tinkling glass.

"Quick!" whispered Dumarest. "On the roof!"

Two guards came around the building as they settled on the edge of the eaves. Their voices were low, slurred by the mist.

"Seems pointless to me. No one ever comes this way at night. Nothing to see or do."

His companion shrugged. "Heeg said to keep watch, so that's what we do. Maybe he's afraid someone will fall into the pool."

"We'd hear them if they did. I've got some prenchet here, want a chew?"

"Well—" The guard hesitated. "Just a little, then. A third of a pod."

They passed and Dumarest relaxed a little. To Tambolt he whispered, "Stay here and keep watch. I'm taking Preleret over the roof."

It was tiled with wide slabs of thin pottery and had no trap or other means of entry. Dumarest sprawled over it, his ear hard to the chill surface. He moved, listened, moved again. A thin hum came from below, machinery of some kind, a device to eliminate the mist from the air inside. Lifting the knife from his boot, he thrust the point between two of the tiles, levered upward, thrust his fingers beneath the edge.

Preleret joined him and together they lifted the slab and set it soundlessly to one side. Warm air gusted from the opening. Beneath lay a blank surface, the softly humming bulk of a machine. Beside it lay the rim of an access trap. It opened to a room bright with reflections. Dumarest dropped through, Preleret following, images flashing all around as they lifted the goggles from their eyes.

"A maze," whispered Preleret. "Mirrors everywhere. What the hell is this, Earl?"

An amusement for those so inclined. Aritficial mirages supplied by electronic means so that those entering would be surrounded by a constantly changing variety of scenes. They would wander, turning, baffled by reflective surfaces, bemused and deceived by visual images.

There were no scenes now, the electronic devices in-operative, but the mirrors remained showing their figures in a dozen different positions. There would be small rooms leading one into the other, twists, turns, angled passages and still more compartments. In one of them must be the boy.

Dumarest lowered the goggles. The reflections vanished to be replaced by the eerie greenness of transmuted infrared light. A point glowed brighter than the rest, a concentrated blob of unrecognizable shape surrounded by a nimbus of light. A living thing radiated heat. The blob could be the boy, the nimbus the room in which he sat.

"There," he said to Preleret. "Lower your goggles and you can see it. Maybe twenty yards ahead."

"Twenty?" Preleret sounded dubious. "Three more like."

Dumarest turned, lifting his goggles. Preleret was looking in the wrong direction. He dived, hitting the man low, knocking him to one side as something burned a hole in the mirror before which he had stood.

"Earl! What—"

The mirror shattered, falling in a rain of glinting crystal. Framed hugely in the opening Heeg Euluch said, "I expected something like this. Well, it seems it was a good idea to check my investment." He lifted his right hand, the laser it contained. "Too bad you couldn't play it straight."

"Thirty thousand," said Dumarest quickly. "Pull that trigger and that's what you lose."

"Begging?"

"Talking sense." Dumarest rose, turning so as to hide the club at his side. "Talking money. You like money, Heeg. That's why you killed to get the boy, why you don't want your partners to know what you have. They'd want a cut and you don't want to give it to them. Thirty thousand and it could be all yours. Yes?"

"No." The laser wavered a little, moving from Dumarest to Preleret and back again. The arc widened as Dumarest edged from the other man. "This is the end of the road for you both. You get it first." The laser jerked at Preleret. "And you get it after you tell me a few things." The gun moved toward Dumarest. "And you'll tell me. That I promise."

Dumarest threw the club.

It flashed, spinning as he jumped aside, slamming

against the laser and knocking it from the big man's hand. Before it had fallen Dumarest was on him, the knife in his hand a glittering arc as it flashed upward at the stomach. It hit, slashed the yellow fabric of the tunic, halted as it struck the mesh beneath. Body armor—he should have expected it.

He sprang backward as the giant hands reached for his eyes, felt the impact of something solid, then fell in a rain of shattered glass. He rose as Heeg reached for the laser, drawing back his arm, sending the knife like an extension of his hand to bury itself deep in the corded throat.

Bleakly he watched the big man die.

"Fast," said Preleret. He had scooped up the laser and held it as he stared wonderingly at Dumarest. "I knew you were quick, but not that quick." He looked at Heeg. "You tried to gut him. You could have got him in the throat to begin with, but you tried to gut him. Why, Earl?"

A farm ruined, a woman killed, a boy stolen, workers slain by imported devils. Jasken gone, others, blood spilled for the sake of gain.

"He asked for it," said Dumarest coldly. "Now let's find the boy."

A solid cube lay in a nest of supporting stanchions approached through a maze of carefully aligned planes of mirrored glass. A bolt fastened the door. Dumarest tore it free and heaved at the portal. It opened to reveal a tiny room, a bed, a single chair, the small figure of a boy who looked up, his eyes wide in the rounded pallor of his face.

"Earl! Is that you?"

"Jondelle!" He came running as Dumarest dropped to one knee, throwing himself into the extended arms, his small weight hard against his chest. "Are you all right?"

"Yes, Earl." The voice was muffled. "I've been very lonely and scared, but I knew you would come to save me. I just knew it." The supreme faith of children which gave to their heroes the attributes of a god. "Are we going home now?"

Up to the roof where Tambolt waited. Down to the ground and over the wall with the laser to cut down all opposition and the raft to waft them to safety.

"Yes," said Dumarest. "We're going home."

CHAPTER

NINETEEN

The wine was as he remembered, red, sweet, cloying to the tongue, but now it seemed to have an added flavor which made it impossible to drink. Dumarest set down the goblet as Akon Batik spoke.

"A successful termination to a dangerous enterprise, Earl. You have reason to be gratified. More, perhaps, than you realize. Now, if you will let me handle the transaction, much profit may be gained by all."

"No," said Dumarest. "The boy is not for sale."

"But—" The jeweler broke off, then shrugged. "A matter of terminology. You, naturally, can claim to be rewarded for what you have done. There have been high expenses and much risk. Those who care for the lad will not be ungrateful. I think five thousand stergals would not be too much to expect. I will give it to you—on taking charge of the boy, of course, and will reclaim it later."

"No." Dumarest looked at his wine. "You mentioned a proposition the first time we met. A job of work to be done. Is it still available?"

"Unfortunately, no."

"The need no longer exists?" Dumarest shrugged. "Of course not. Neema is safe now. She no longer wants someone to go to Melevgan and rescue her. That was the proposition, wasn't it? That I should go and collect her so that you could collect fat profits at no risk. The fee, her jewels—you are a shrewd man, Akon Batik."

"One who takes advantage of an opportunity, Earl. If that is to be shrewd, then I must confess to the fault. But you must admit that, as far as you were concerned, I proved of service."

"Tambolt," agreed Dumarest. "A man sent to me because he was a man I could use. But I think he was a little more than that. Your agent to keep an eye on things, to work on your behalf. Unfortunately you didn't know him all that well. Tambolt would sell his own mother for gain. He added, "I think he believes I tricked him. I promise him half of what I would get for the boy—which was half of exactly nothing. He had to be content with his thir of the agreed profit."

"The reward—"

"I didn't go after Jondelle for reward! I went becaus —well, never mind."

"A promise," said the jeweler softly. "Your word. Som times I am amazed at the stupidity of men. What wa the boy to you? Why did you have to risk your life t get him? To kill and have men killed. And never wa the boy in any real danger. Time would have cured al An exchange, as you have said, the passing of money an he would have been returned. It was simply a matter c negotiation."

"As you say—a matter of negotiation."

"Exactly. So why should you deny yourself the chanc of gain? Five thousand, ten High passages, a small fortun Shall we drink to it?"

Dumarest said, "No. I do not care for your wine. has a taste I can't stomach."

"A taste?" The jeweler frowned. "You suspect poison"

Dumarest rose and moved from the chair where laser if any, would be aimed. He said, coldly, "Not poison-vileness. A man cannot be blamed for his nature, but som men go too far. Money becomes their god, their on reason for being, and, when it does, they stop being huma They become like the things found under an ove turned stone. Spiders sitting in a web of intrigue, manip lating men and women, arranging, hinting, offering, doir nothing but creating desolation. I should kill you. I shou bury a knife in your throat as I did Heeg Euluch. Yo arranged with him to steal the boy. You contacted Neen by radio and there are radios in Charne. Maybe Elray w first approached, or he could even have contacted you— doesn't matter now. When you failed to get him in the cit you obtained other help. Fast rafts, willing men, agents do your bidding. Or perhaps you had everything arrang in case of initial failure.

"You are shrewd and clever—and you deserve to d But I won't kill you. I don't have to. Time will do th soon enough. You're old, Akon Batik. Too old to given the mercy of a quick end. So sit and wait for yo

ones to stiffen and your faculties to weaken. Until, maybe, someone treats you exactly as you treat others."

Outside the air was clean, invigorating after the nest in
which the jeweler sat. Dumarest hailed a cab and was
driven to the hotel. It was a big place, the best in Sargone.
Neema met him as he entered the suite. She was radiant,
her arm healed, neatly and quietly dressed in a gown which
covered her from neck to ankles.

"Preleret's gone, Earl. He's taken his cask and his
woman and gone riding High. To Rodyne, I think. He said
that you didn't need thanks, but he left them just the
same."

"A good man," said Dumarest. "He'll be happy."

"As I will be."

"In Urmile?"

"On some other world. I've had enough of Ourelle, Earl.
Now that you don't need me to look after the boy—" She
paused and said, softly, "Earl?"

Gently he shook his head. "No, Neema."

"Well, I asked." She managed to smile. "You're not
a man to be held by any woman, Earl. I know that, but
I had to try. Did you see the jeweler?"

"Yes, but I learned nothing new. I guess I lost my
temper. It was a mistake, perhaps, but I couldn't help
it."

"Did you kill him?"

"No."

"Then you didn't lose your temper. You simply told
him a few things he should have known. And, perhaps,
verified things you had suspected." She came very close,
resting her hand on his arm. "I'll be off now. The boy
is in the other room with the monk and his people. I don't
suppose I'll ever see you again, but I'm going to think of
you often. So good-bye, my dear, and may good fortune
attend each step you take."

"And may your life be full of gladness."

She kissed him once and then was gone, leaving the
room strangely empty, a hint of her perfume hanging in the
air as if she had become a disembodied ghost haunting him
with vague regrets of what might have been.

A woman, a home, a son, perhaps, like Jondelle.
Drawing a deep breath Dumarest went into the room where
the boy waited with Brother Elas and two others.

He sat on the edge of the bed, very busy with his

beads, running them through his fingers, lifting them to his ear as if to listen to forgotten voices. Toys lay beside him, a fluffy, round-eared, bright-eyed creature with snub nose and cheerful smile almost as large as himself. A spaceship which could be dismantled and reassembled. A colorscope which showed endless patterns at the touch of a button, the shapes rearranging themselves beneath directed compulsion. Some books, blocks of transparent plastic containing variable images, a knife.

Jondelle lifted it and threw it clumsily at the pillow. The plastic blade bent and left the material unharmed.

"One day, Earl, I'm going to learn to throw it just like you."

"One day," he said.

"And then no one will be able to take me away again. They won't be able to hurt anyone like they did Elray and Makgar." The full bottom lip trembled a little. "I shall kill them if they try. Oh, Earl! Why did they do it? Why?"

Dumarest held him, feeling the small body shake, the wetness of sudden tears. The adult words had gone, the calm behavior, now there was only a very small and bewildered child.

He said, "It's all right, Jondelle. Everything's going to be all right from now. A bad thing has happened, but it will pass. You have had bad dreams, haven't you? Well, sometimes life is like a bad dream. But you forget dreams and you can forget unhappiness. So you must try to do that. You promise?"

"I promise."

"Good. Go with Brother Elas now and wash your face."

"You'll be here when I come back?"

"Yes," said Dumarest. "I'll be here."

He rose as the monk ushered the boy from the room, looking at the others for the first time. A man and woman, neither young, both blond, blue-eyed, looking as if they were brother and sister.

"Tharg Hamsen," said the man, extending his hand. "And my wife, Wilma."

Dumarest took the extended hand and pressed it.

"You know the old customs; good." The man smiled, then became grave. "To talk of thanks at a time like this is to use empty words. You have found our grandson— what can I say?"

"Nothing." Dumarest looked from one to the other

eeing the similarities, the telltale marks of blood-relation-
hip. Selective inbreeding, he guessed, common on many
vorlds among races which aimed at a desired goal. But
either would have chosen Makgar for their son's wife.
'he had been totally different from what they would have
ccepted as a desirable mate. Carefully he said, "Your
on must have presented you with quite a problem."

"Jak?" The man frowned. "No, he was a good boy. I
annot understand what you mean."

"You are obtuse, Tharg." His wife with her woman's
ntuition had grasped Dumarest's meaning. "Earl is being
lelicate. But you are mistaken, my friend. The woman
'ou knew as Makgar was not Jondelle's mother. She bore
im, true, but while Jak provided the seed she did not
rovide the egg. You understand?"

"A plant?"

"Yes. The fertilized egg taken from the womb of one
voman and planted in the womb of another. Tharg?"

"Jak and May were on Veido, a working honeymoon.
'he was newly pregnant and they were as happy as a couple
an be. There was an accident, a ground car—the details
lon't matter. Jak was killed instantly, May was injured,
lying, and with her would die the child. The child and
he precious genes it carried!" He paused, breathing deeply,
ontinuing in a calmer tone. "Perhaps you don't under-
tand. We are inbred as you can see and that tends to lead
o a degree of sterility. Jak was our only child, the last
f his line. If his genes were lost, it would set back a
rogram for unknown years. The work of a hundred gene-
ations lost because of a trick of fate. I—"

"They were connected with a scientific establishment on
'eido," said Wilma as he broke off. "Kamar Ragnack—
Makgar—was a technician attached to the medical side.
he and May were friends and she volunteered to have
he fertilized egg transplanted into her womb. It was done.
May died. Time passed and the baby, Jondelle, was born.
t is essential to the well-being of a newly born child to
tay with its mother and so we arranged for them to occupy
small house close to the city. And then, one day, the
voman vanished taking the child with her."

Dumarest said, "Was there duress?"

"None." The woman looked down at her hands. They
vere clenched. Slowly she unfolded them. "I can under-
tand," she said. "As a mother I can understand. And

Jondelle was not a normal child. He was bred to develo
a high sympathy-reaction, a survival trait which we co
sider to be important. It was just that Kamar couldn't be
to part with him. She wanted him beside her, to keep fo
always. The normal reaction of any woman toward th
child of her body. I can understand—but I don't fin
it easy to forgive."

"Six years," said Tharg heavily. "Asking, searchin
offering rewards. A long time."

Long enough for men like Akon Batik to have scente
the bait. For Elray to have realized the value of what h
had. For a home to be disrupted and the boy used as
pawn.

Dumarest said, "Was there another reason why Makga
could have taken the child? To protect him, perhaps?"

"From whom? Us?"

A suspicion, but one which was always with him. "A
there cybers on Veido?"

"Yes," said Tharg. "There are."

"And on your own world?"

"Kreem? No."

"Perhaps you had better make sure there never are,
said Dumarest. "The Cyclan are always interested i
potential advantage. A boy, bred to hold the qualities yo
say, would be most useful. Well, you have him . . . tak
care of him."

"Need you say that?" The man sighed. "I understan
The galaxy is full of enemies and who is Jondelle not t
have his share? But he will be protected; have no fear o
that. We know how to take care of our own. And we kno
how to reward those who wish us well."

"Money," said the woman. "But more than tha
Something you value more than the cost of a few Hig
passages. Brother Elas told us of your search. He learne
of it from the records on Hope. Perhaps we can help yo
to find your home."

"Earth?"

"The legendary world," said Tharg quietly. "Som
believe in it, most do not. There are those who are con
vinced it was the home of the human race. A plac
from which they fled in terror." His voice deepene
contained echoes which rolled like drums. "From terro
they fled to find new places on which to expiate thei

sins. Only when cleansed will the race of Man be again united."

The creed of the Original People. Dumarest turned from where he stood beside the window, staring, mind burning with a sudden suspicion. The Original People. These? Were they members of the cult? It so, they would never admit it and he would lose anything he hoped to gain by pressing too hard. Already they had said too much if they followed the ancient ways.

"I have investigated old legends," said Tharg blandly. "From what I can discover, Earth must lie somewhere in the seventh decan. It is a planet circling a yellow, G-type star. It should not be too difficult to hire a computer to determine the exact position of each such star in that area."

Another clue to add to the rest. The final one, perhaps, to solve the problem of where the planet of his birth was to be found.

The door to the bathroom opened and Brother Elas ushered Jondelle into the room. It was time to say good-bye.

"I wondered if you'd be here, Earl. But you promised and I knew that you would. Earl, can't you come with us?"

"No." Dumarest dropped to one knee as he had done once before, feeling again the small body in his arms, the weight against his chest. "I've other things to do, Jondelle, and so have you."

"Shall I see you again?"

"Perhaps. Who can tell what the future will bring? But I shall always remember you."

"And I you, Earl." He stepped back, very small but very upright, his square shoulders framed against the bed and the toys his grandparents had brought. The people who would give him all the love and security he would need. The things every child should have by right. He held out his hand, an odd gesture recently learned.

"Good-bye, Earl."

Dumarest took the little hand, squeezed it. "Good-bye, son."

Beyond the window lay the city, the spacefield, the ships which would carry him on his way. They seemed blurred and he guessed it must be raining.